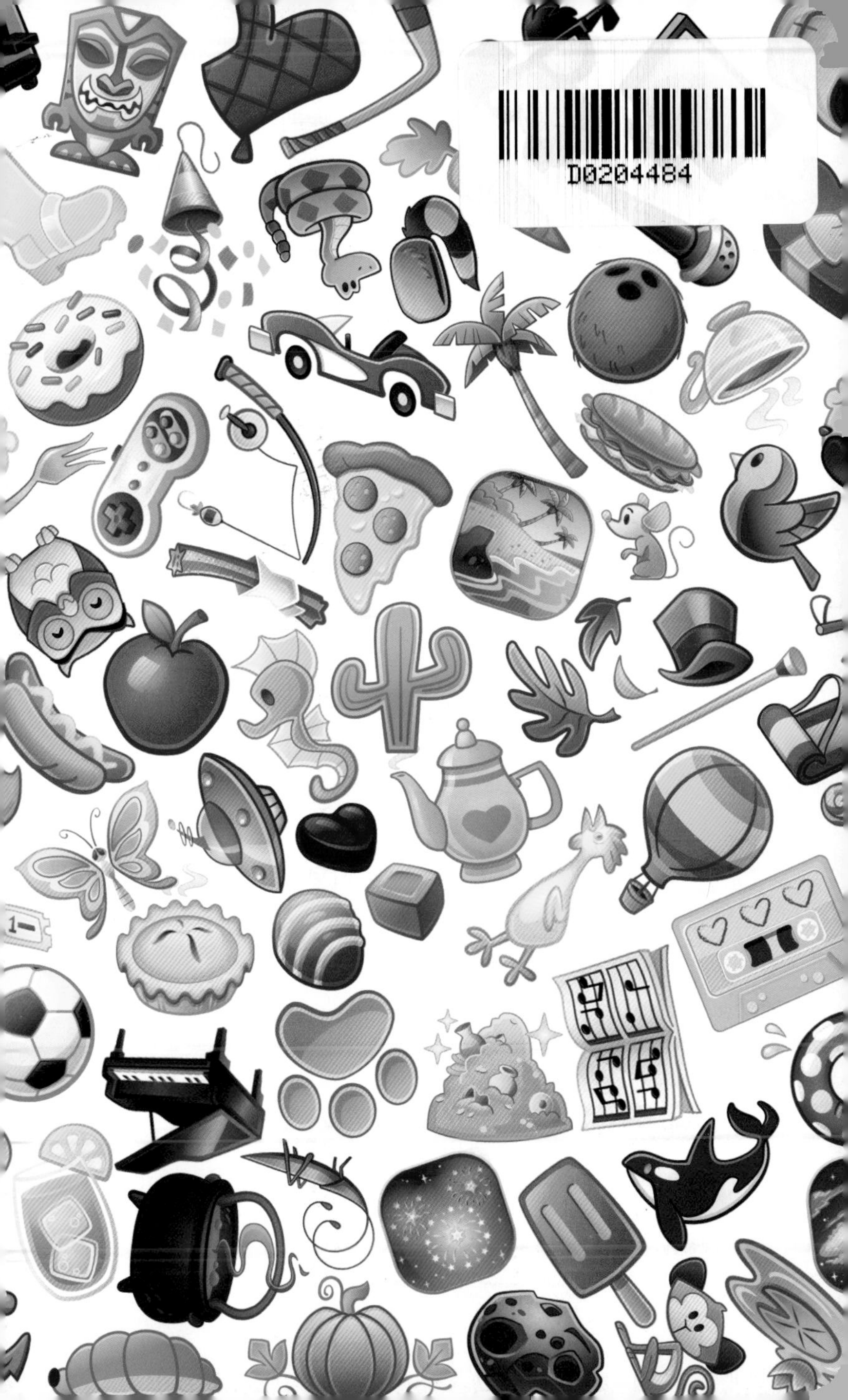

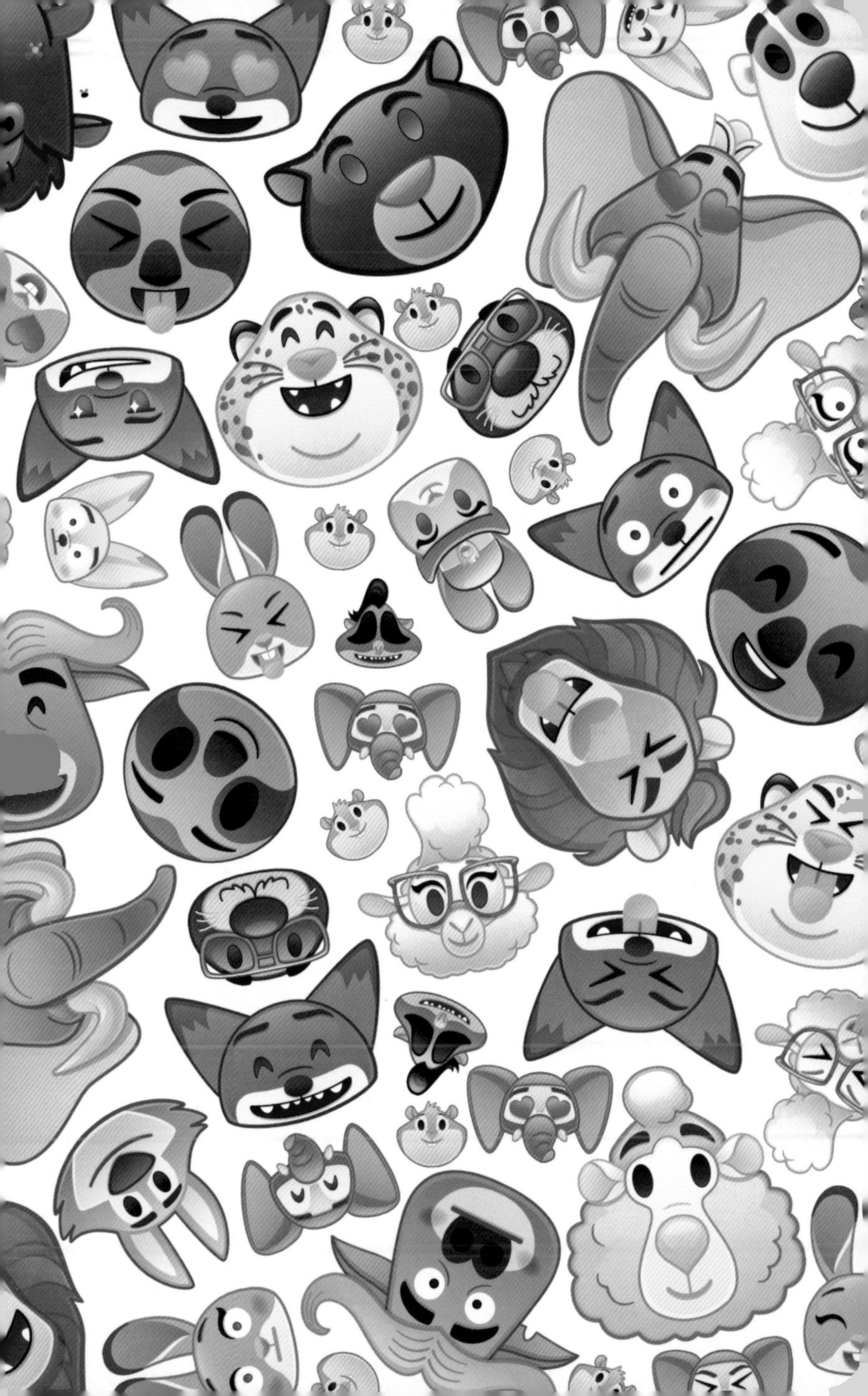

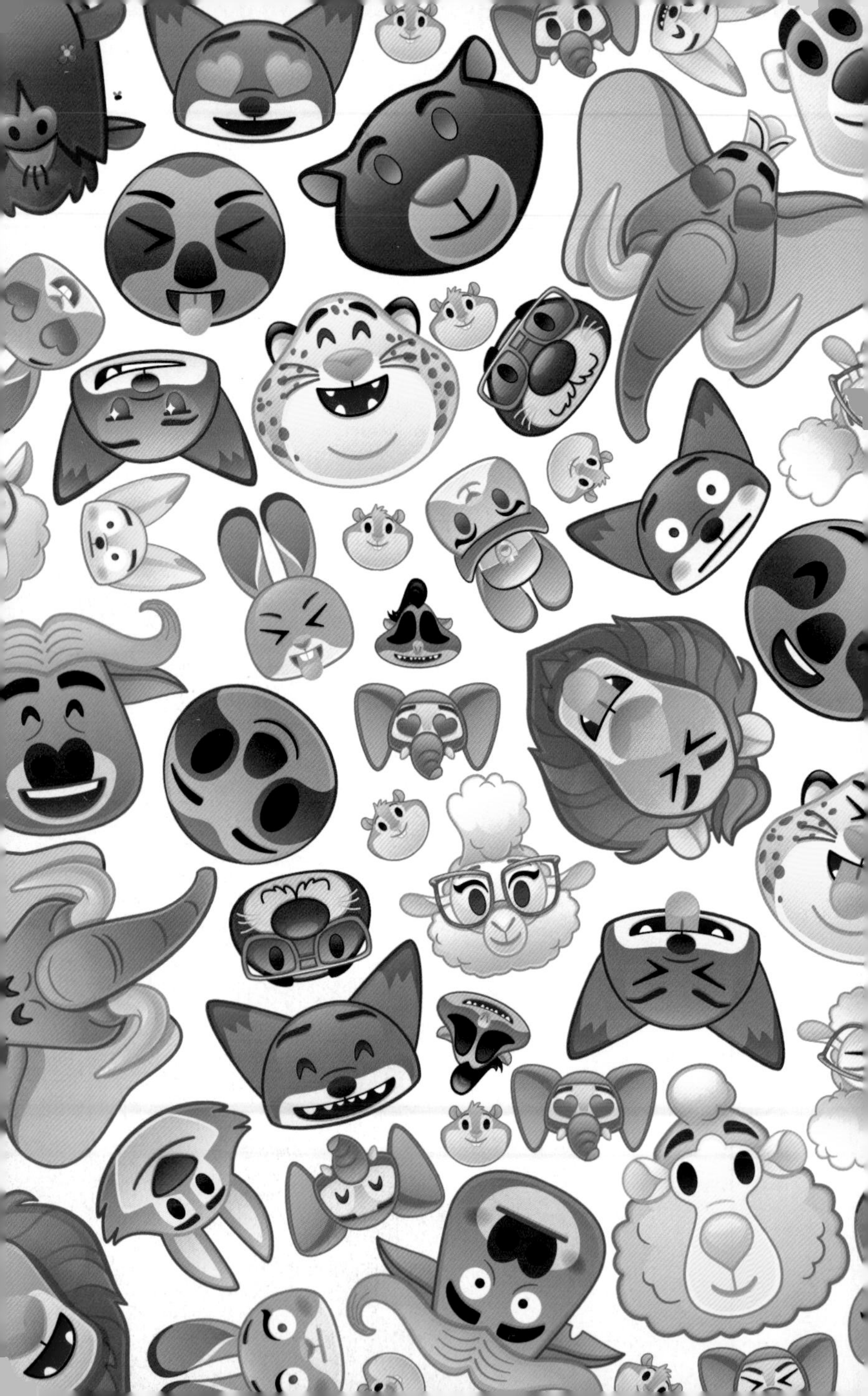

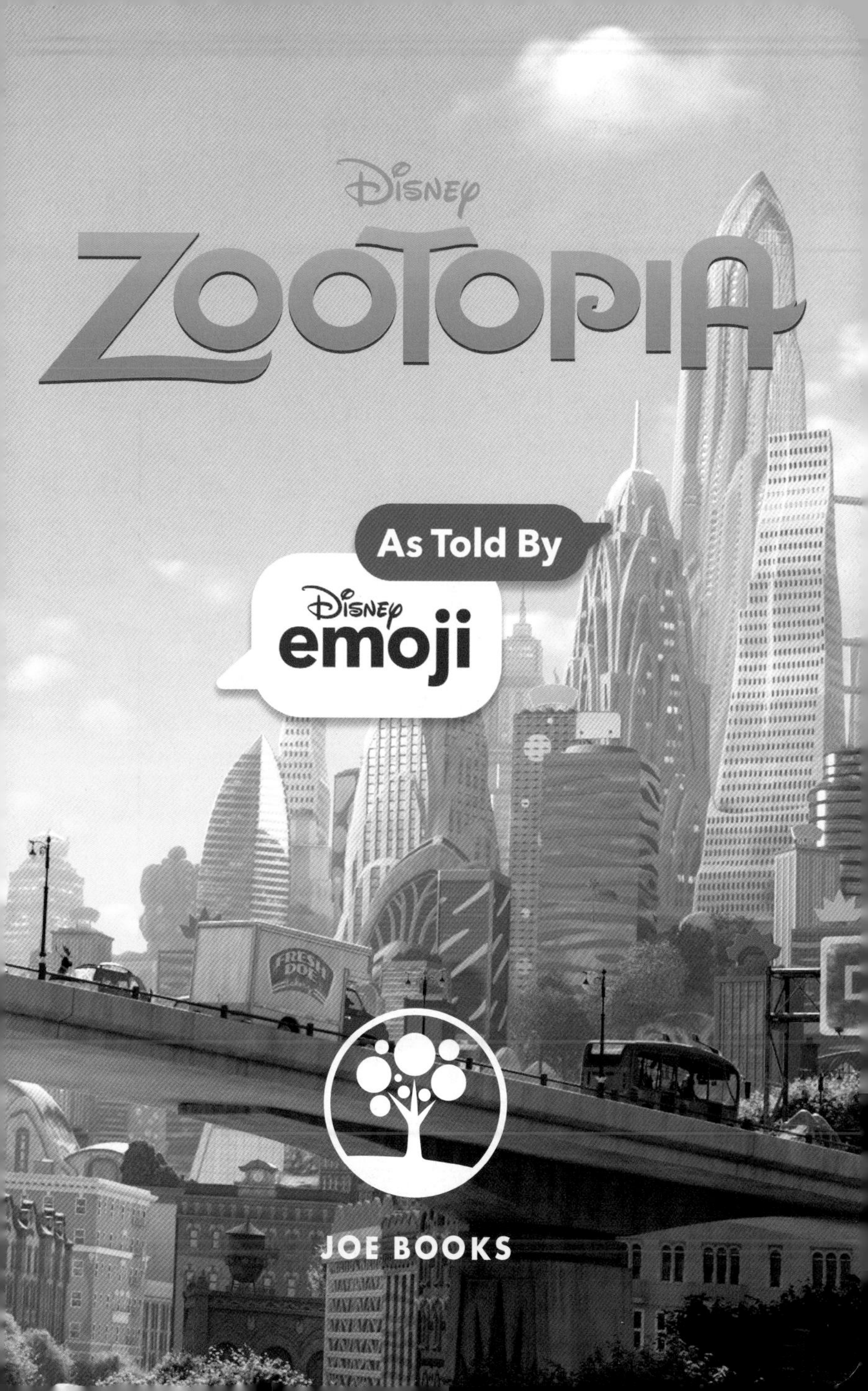

Disney

Zootopia

As Told By

Disney emoji

JOE BOOKS

Published simultaneously in the United States and Canada by Joe Books Ltd,
489 College Street, Suite 203, Toronto, ON M6G 1A5

www.joebooks.com

First Joe Books edition: September 2017

Print ISBN: 978-1-77275-535-0

ebook ISBN: 978-1-77275-789-7

Library and Archives Canada Cataloguing in Publication
information is available upon request

Printed and bound in Canada
1 3 5 7 9 10 8 6 4 2

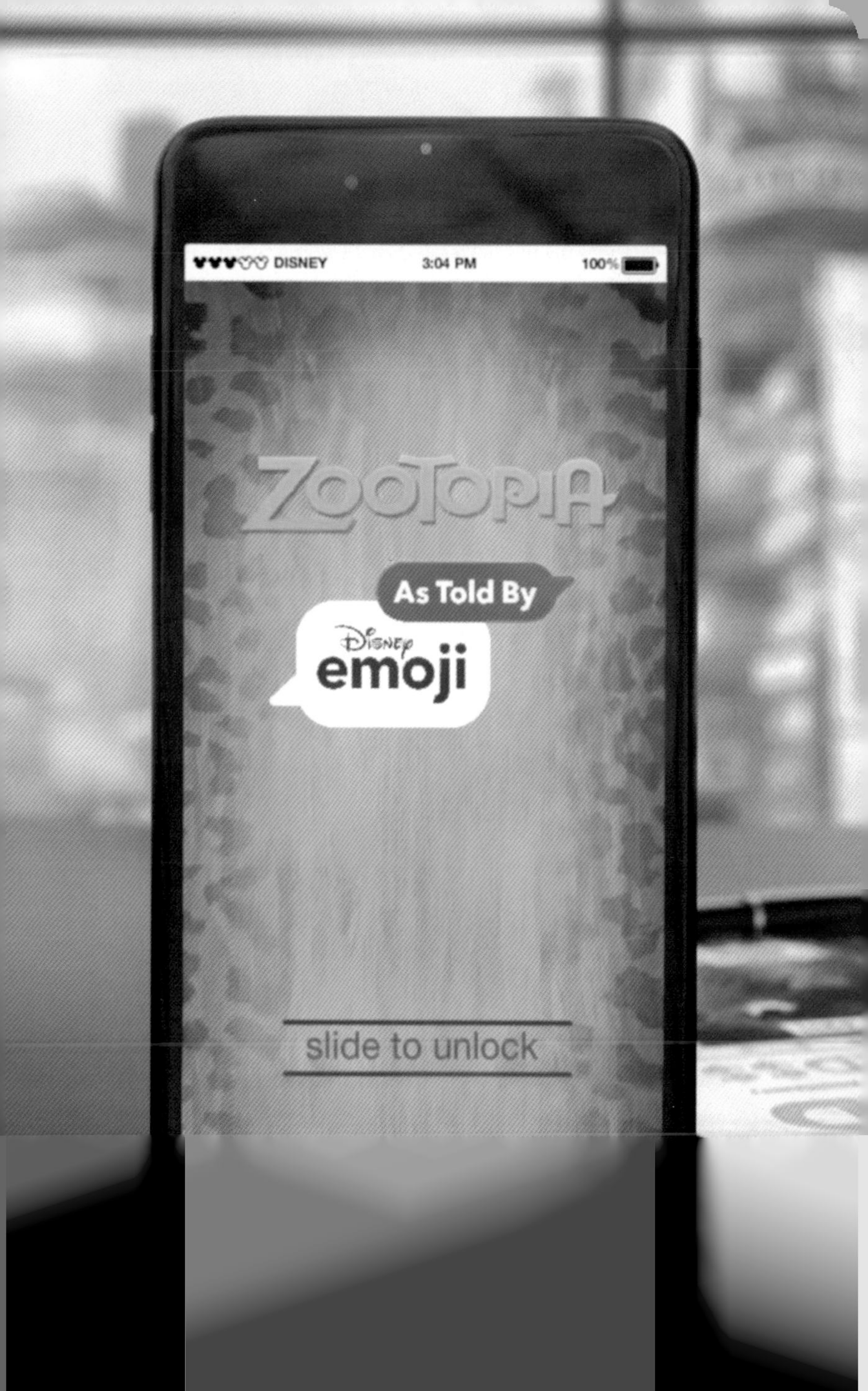
DISNEY
3:04 PM
100%
ZOOTOPIA
As Told By
Disney
emoji
slide to unlock

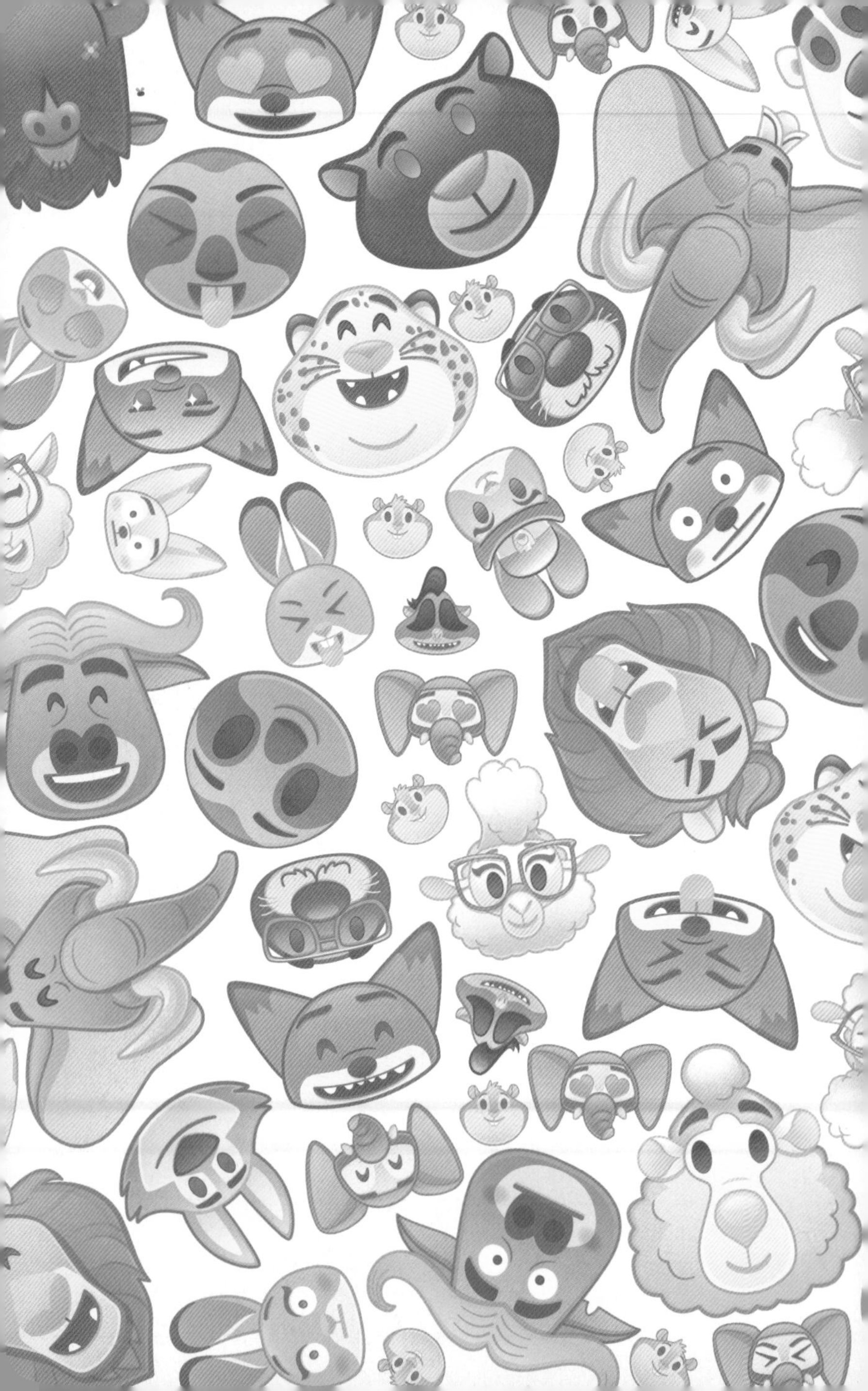

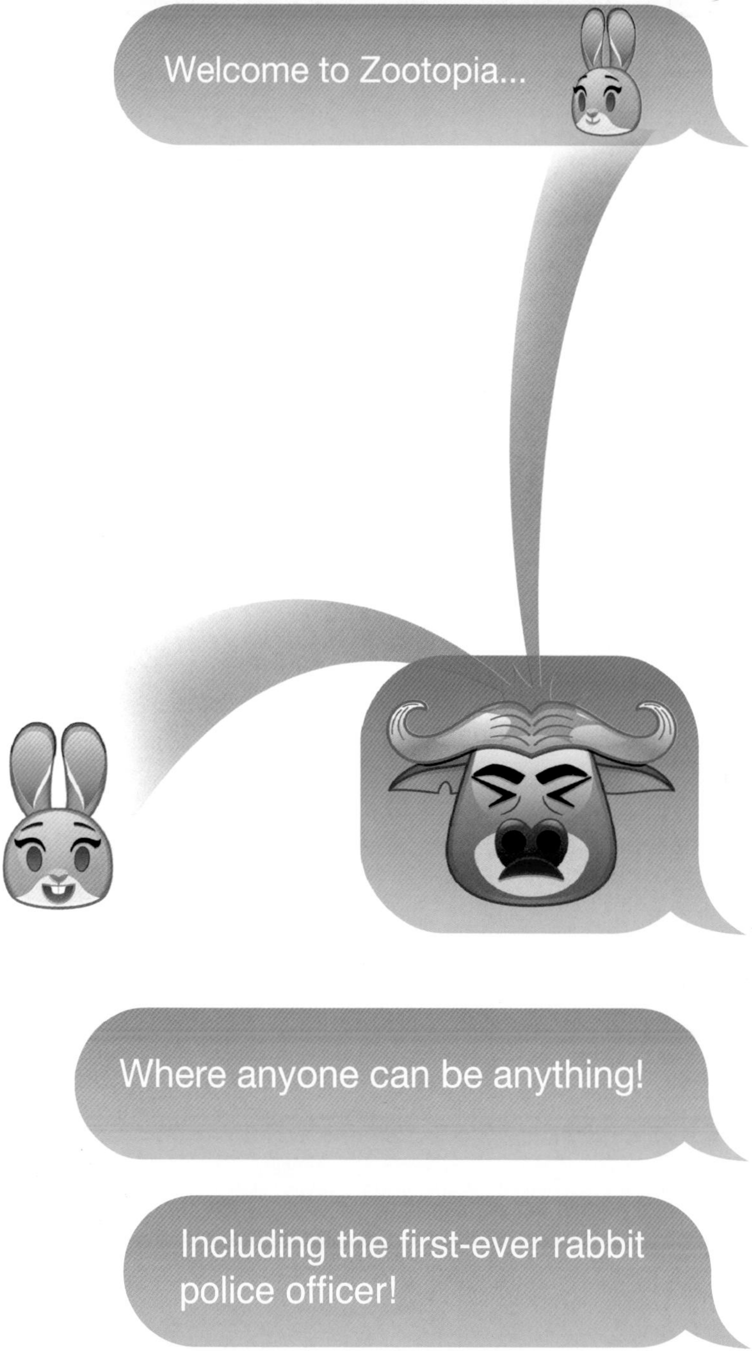
Welcome to Zootopia...
Where anyone can be anything!
Including the first-ever rabbit police officer!

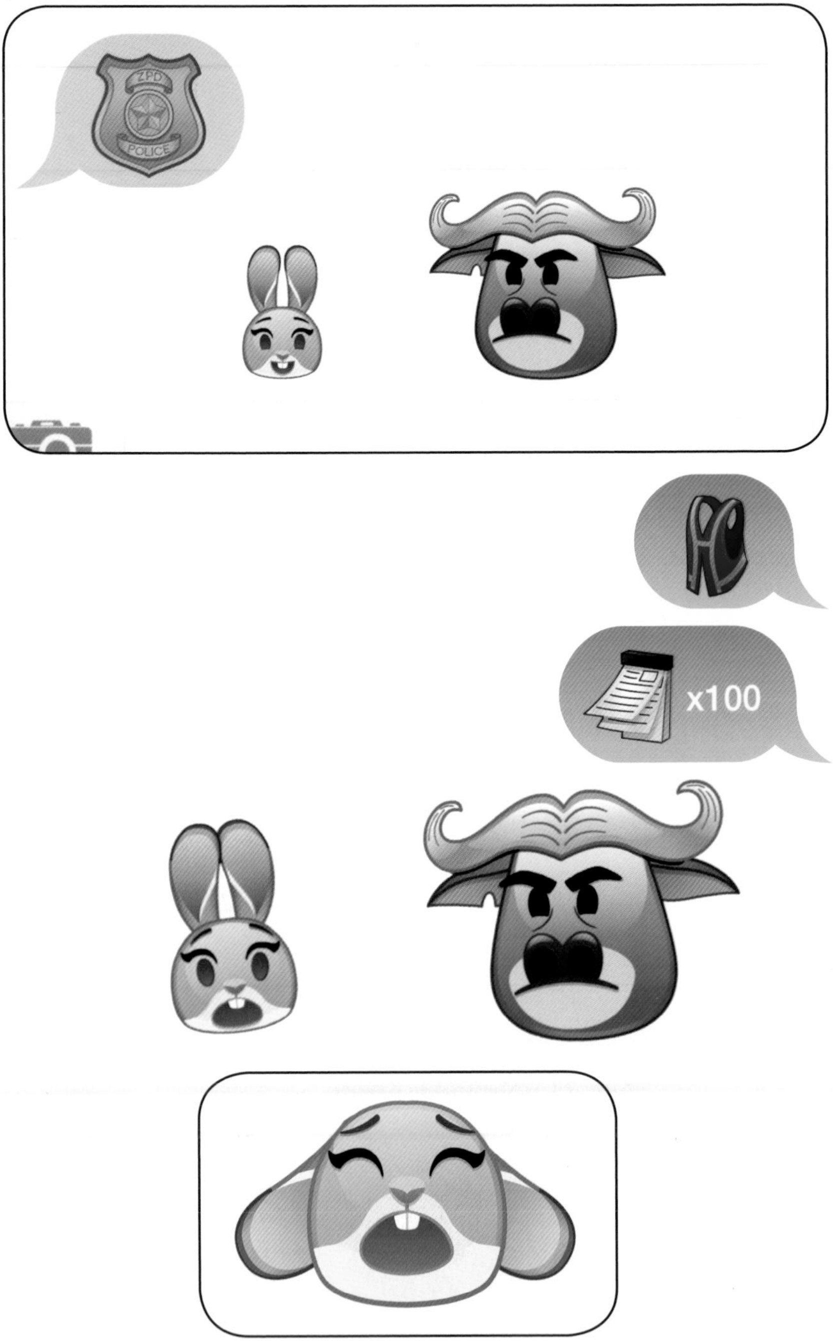
ZPD
POLICE
x100

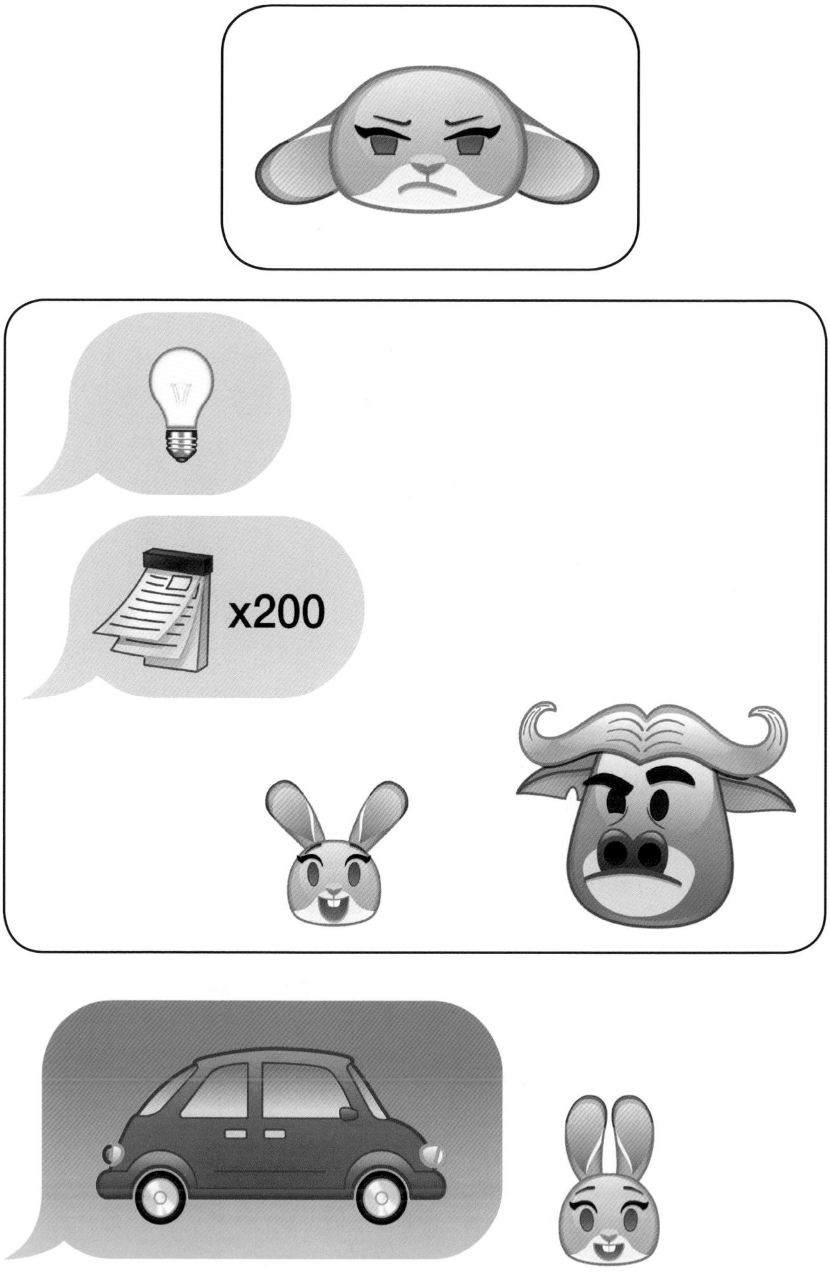
x200

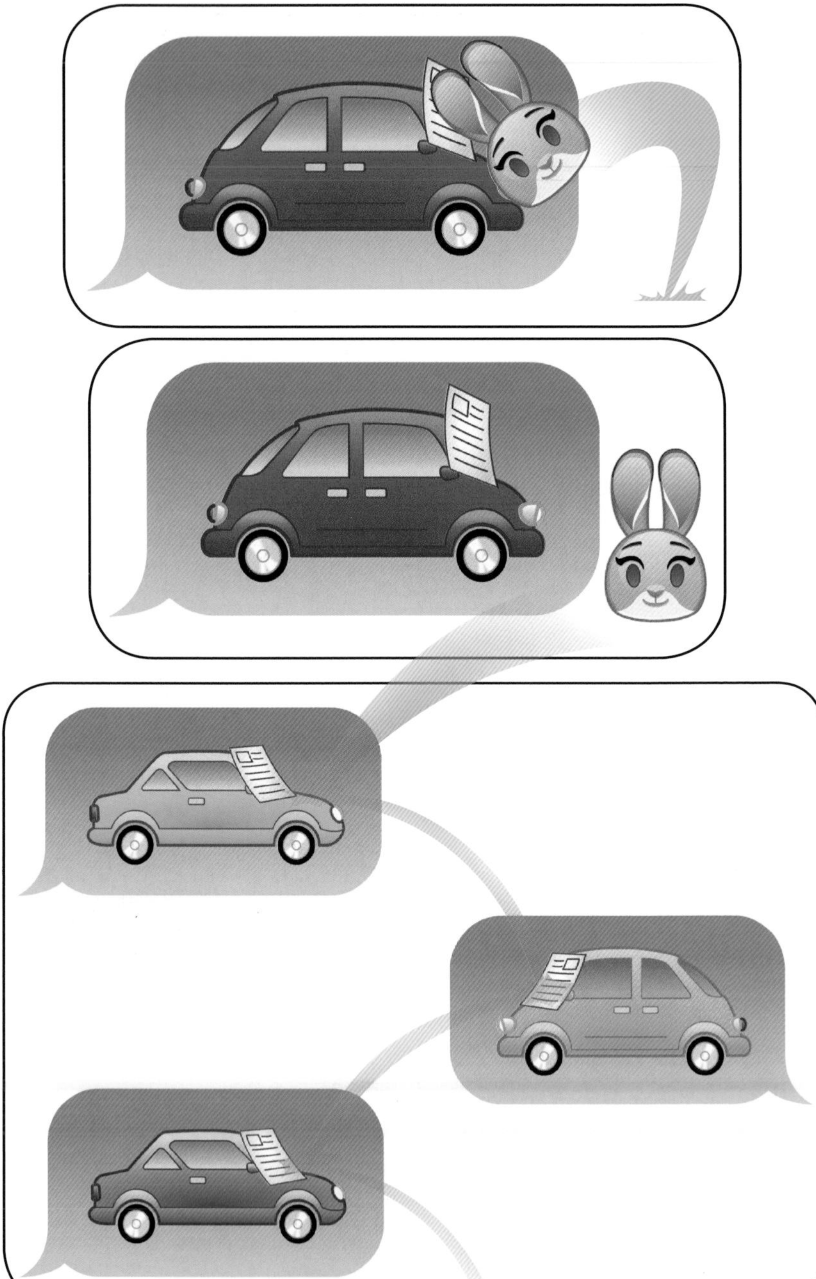

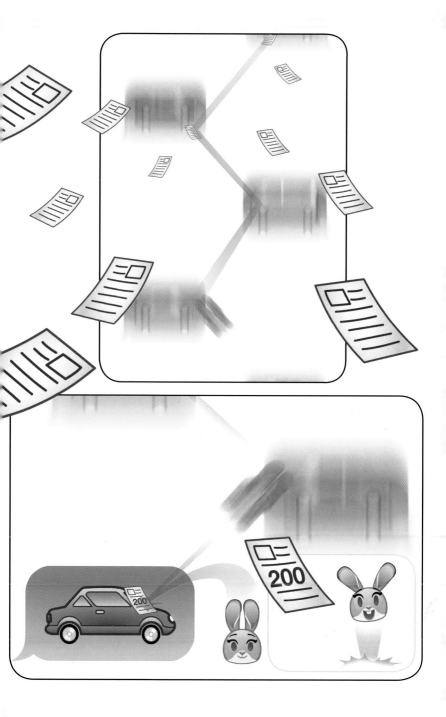

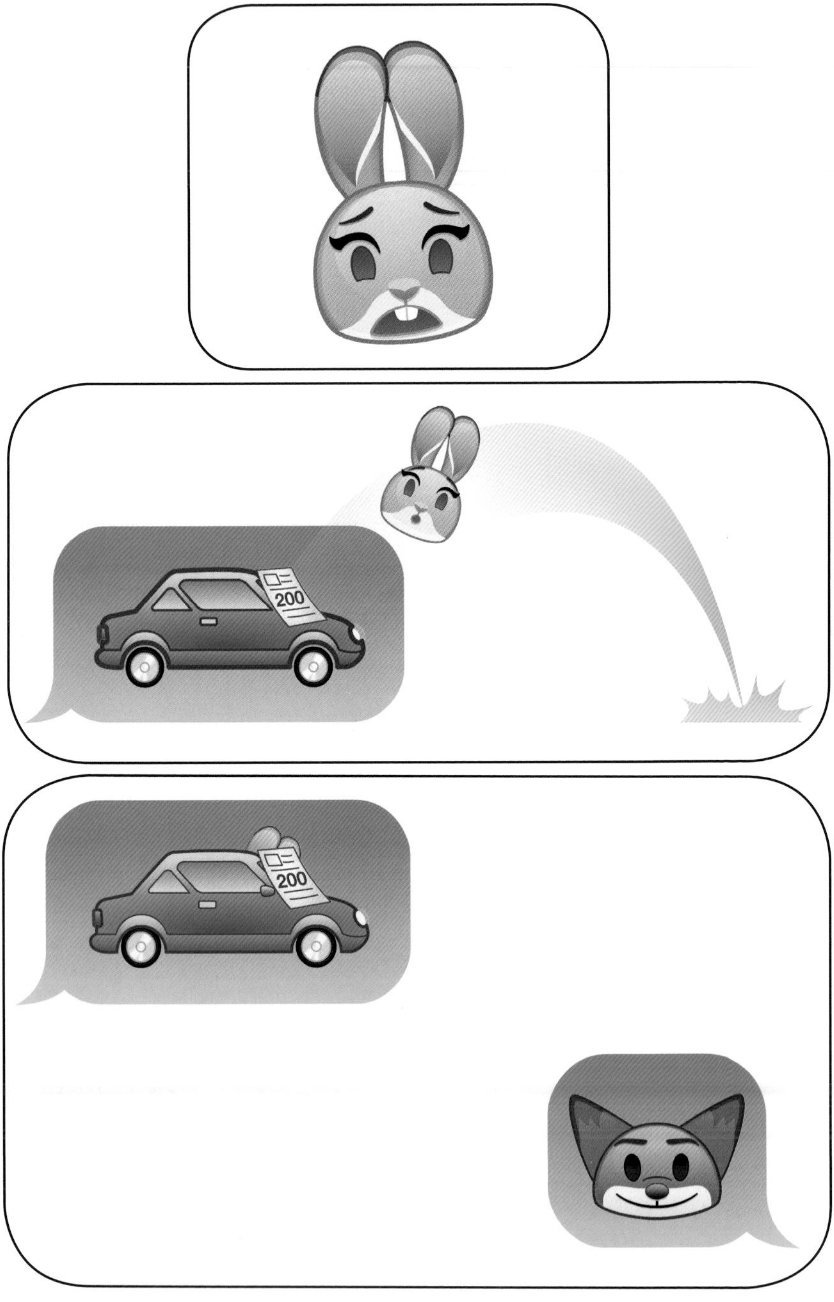
200
200

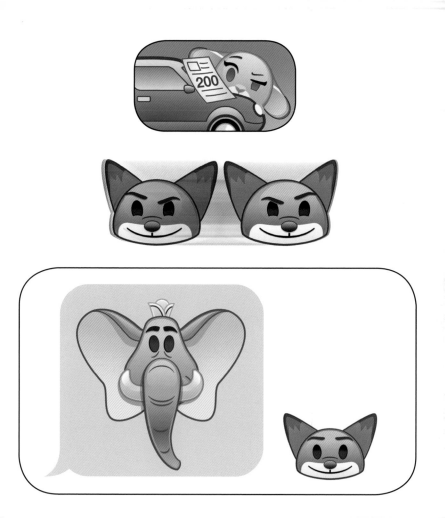

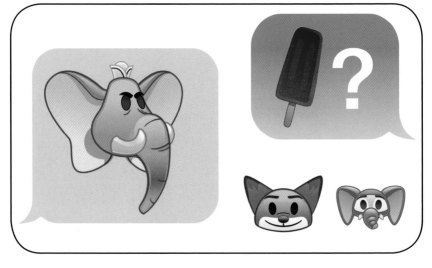

SEND

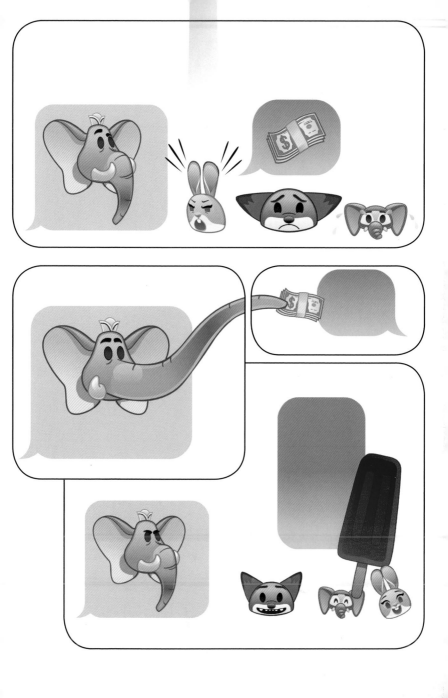

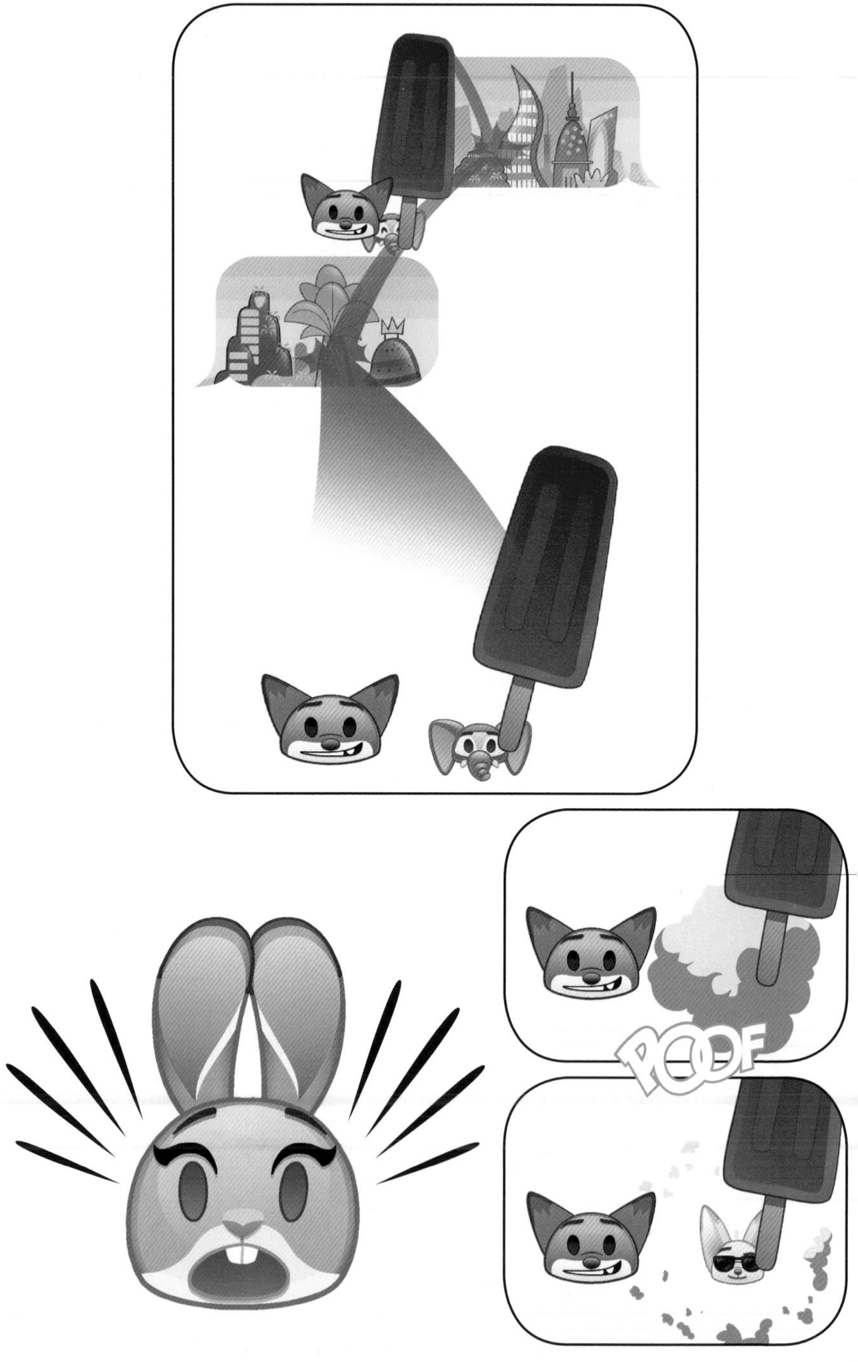
POOF

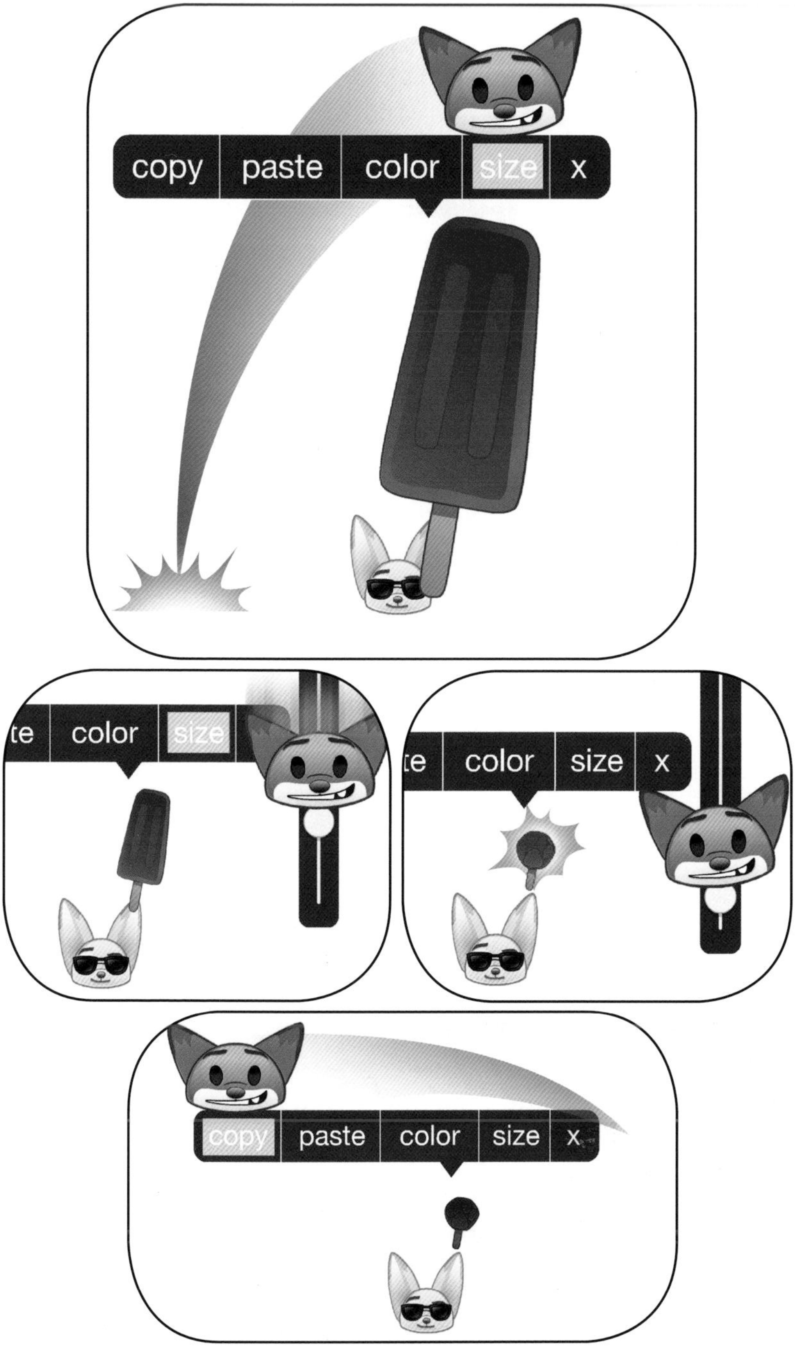
copy paste color size x
te color size
te color size x
copy paste color size x

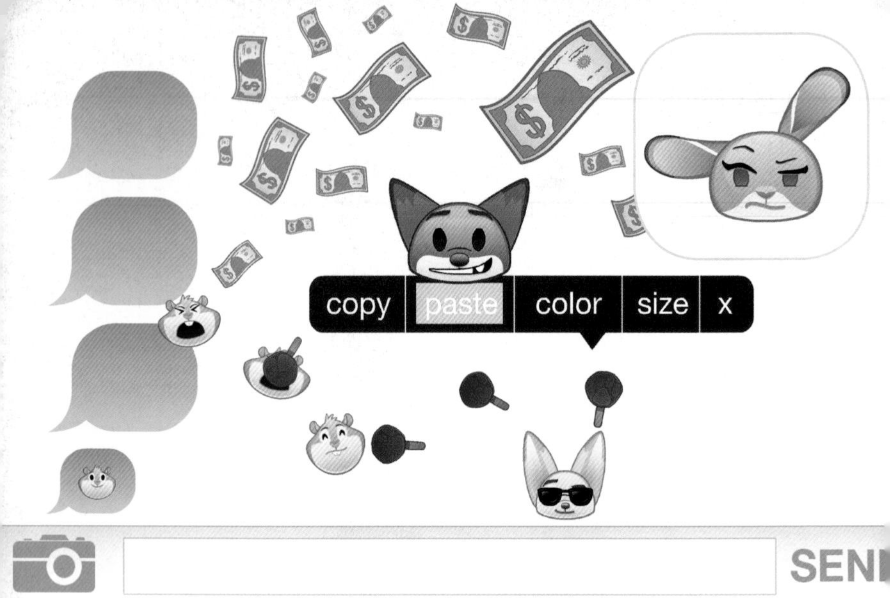
copy
paste
color
size
x

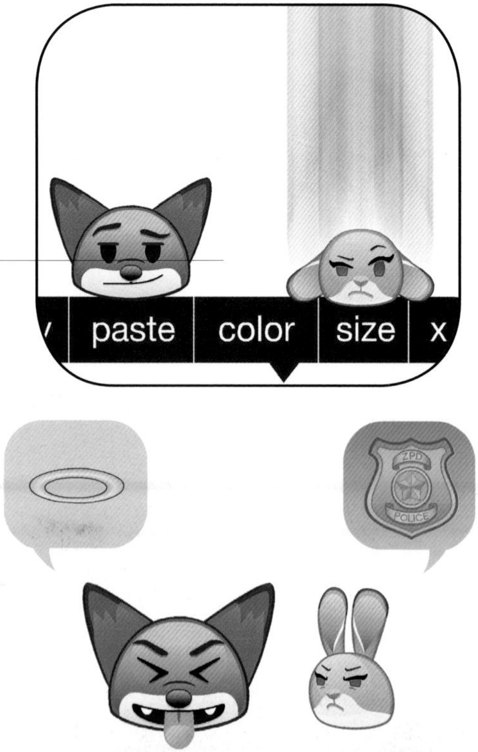
paste
color
size
x
ZPD
POLICE

BZZZZ T

Otter Alert:

MISSING OTTER!
(SAVANNAH CENTRAL)

OK

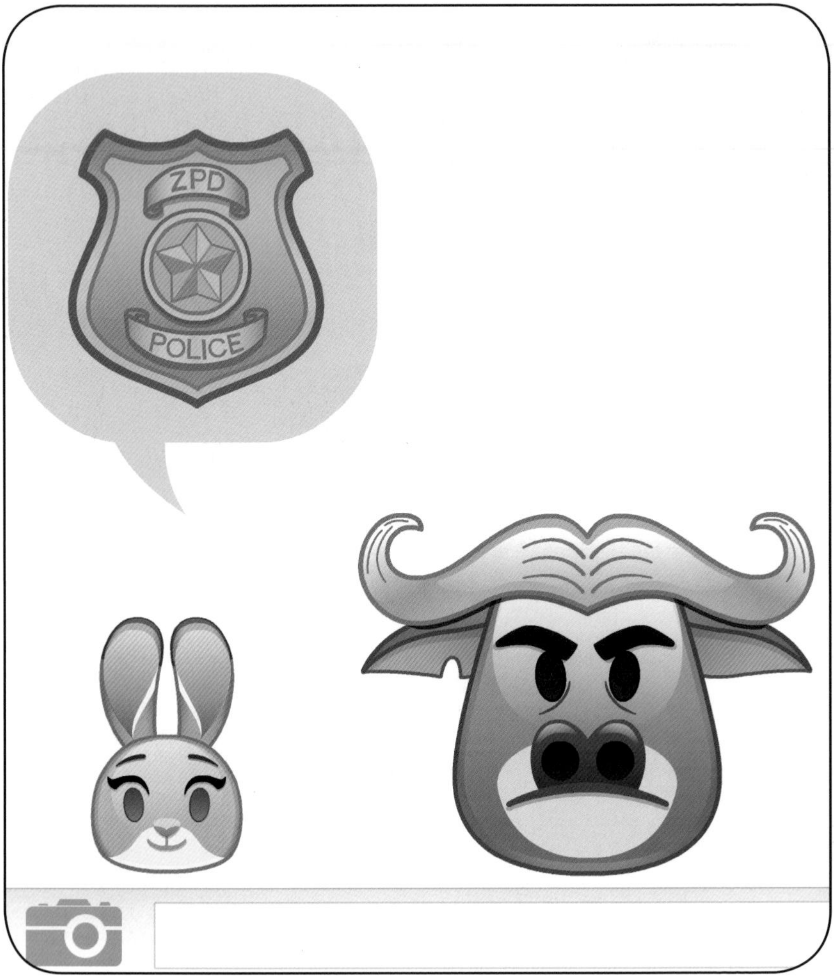
ZPD
POLICE

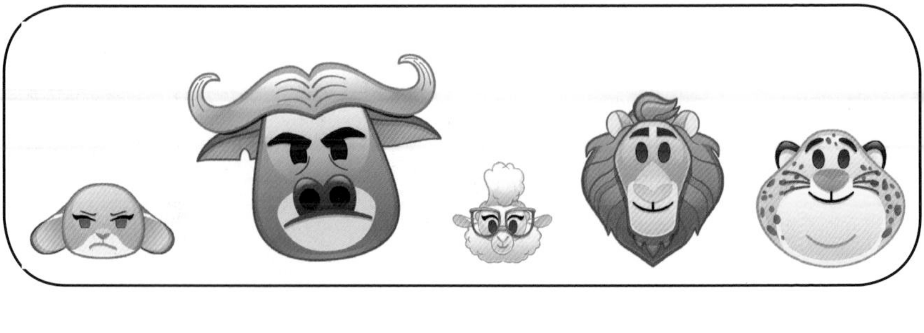

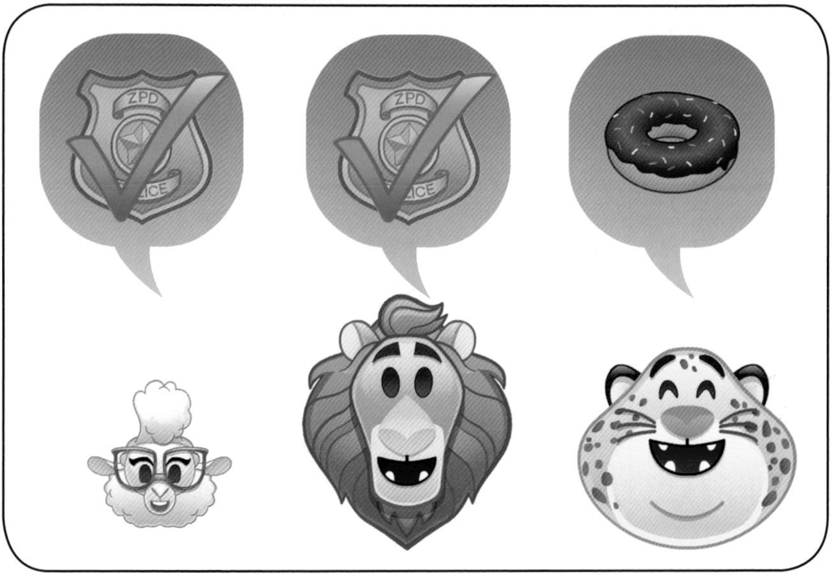
ZPD
ZPD

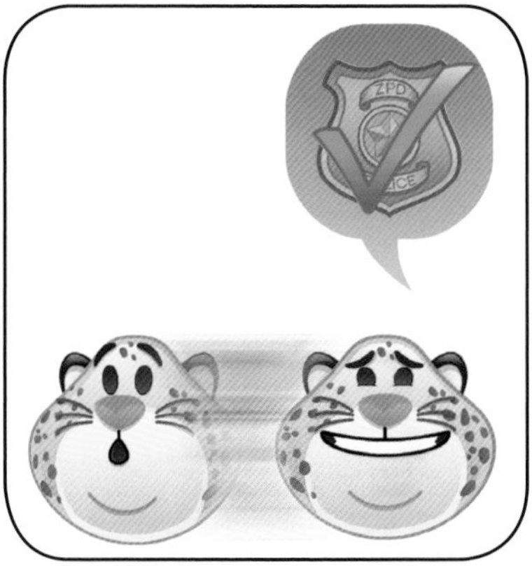
ZPD

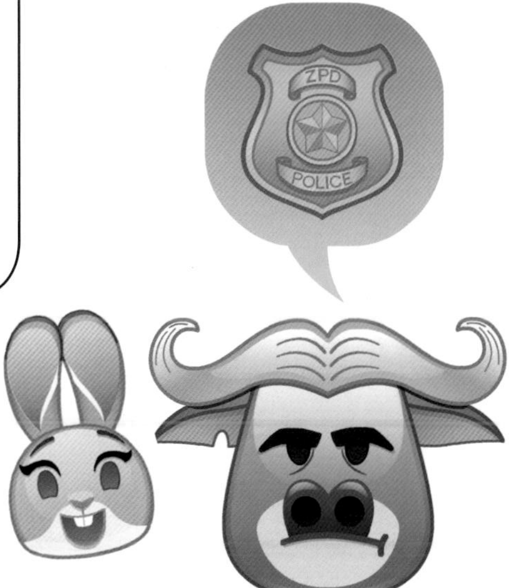
ZPD
POLICE

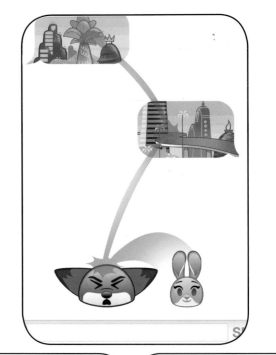

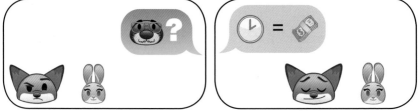

Tax Evasion Confession
----||-|-||-|||||-|-|-||--||--- 0:12

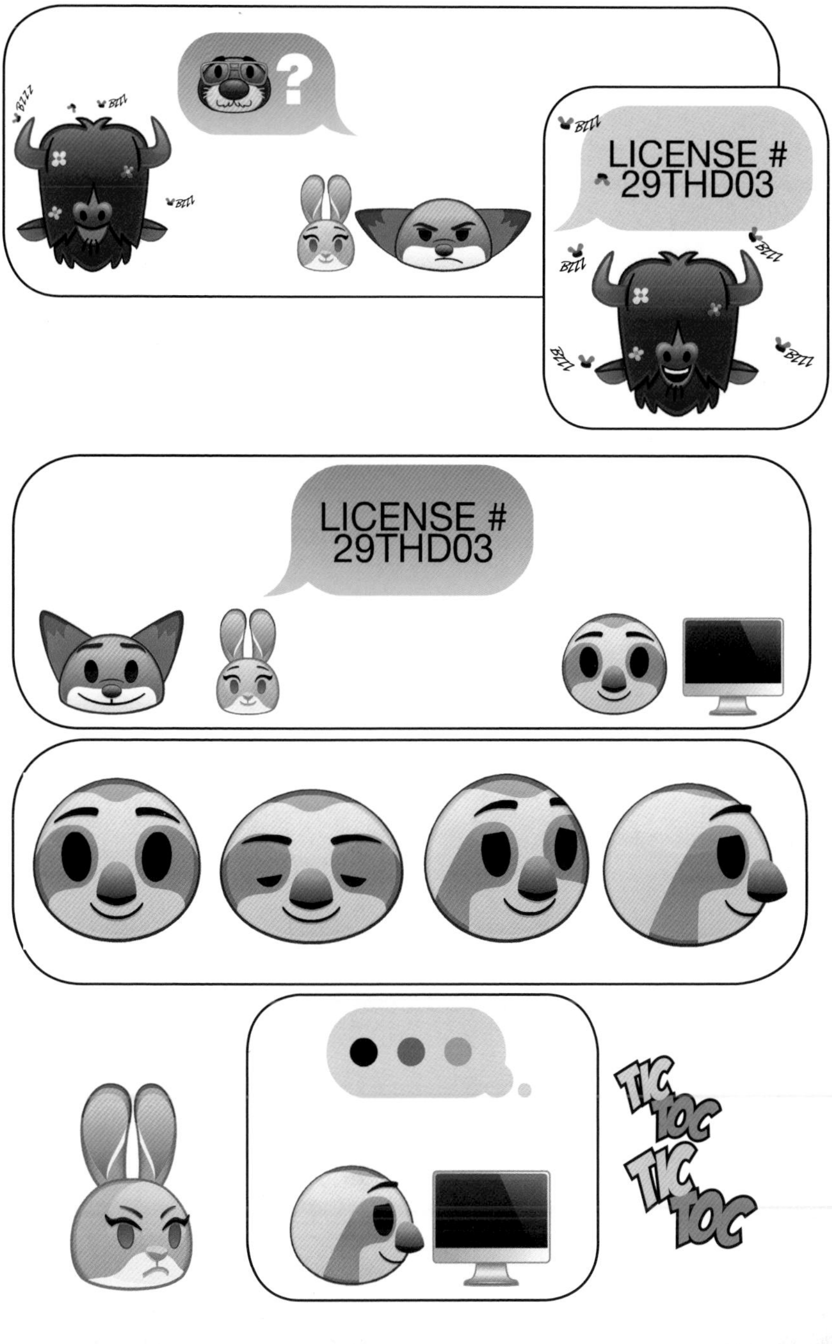
LICENSE #
29THD03
LICENSE #
29THD03
TIC
TOC
TIC
TOC

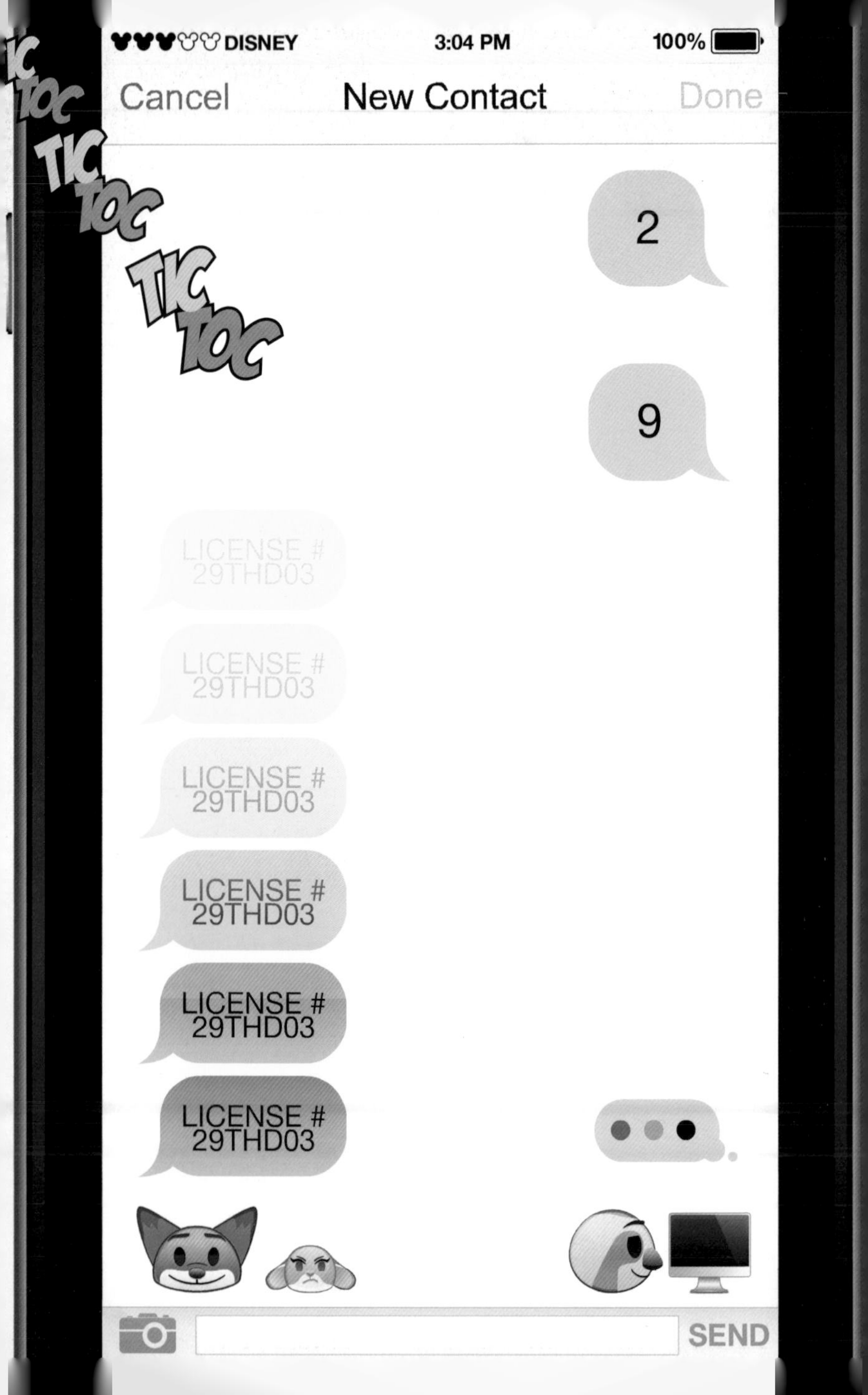
DISNEY
3:04 PM
100%
Cancel
New Contact
Done
TIC TOC
TIC TOC
TIC TOC
2
9
LICENSE # 29THD03
LICENSE # 29THD03
LICENSE # 29THD03
LICENSE # 29THD03
LICENSE # 29THD03
LICENSE # 29THD03
SEND

CALENDAR

31

Notification:
Six Hours Later

In Tundratown...

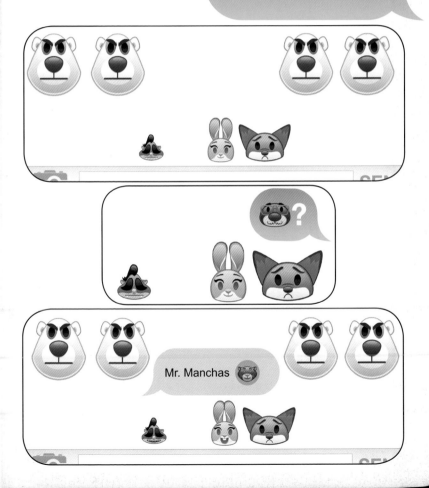

Mr. Manchas

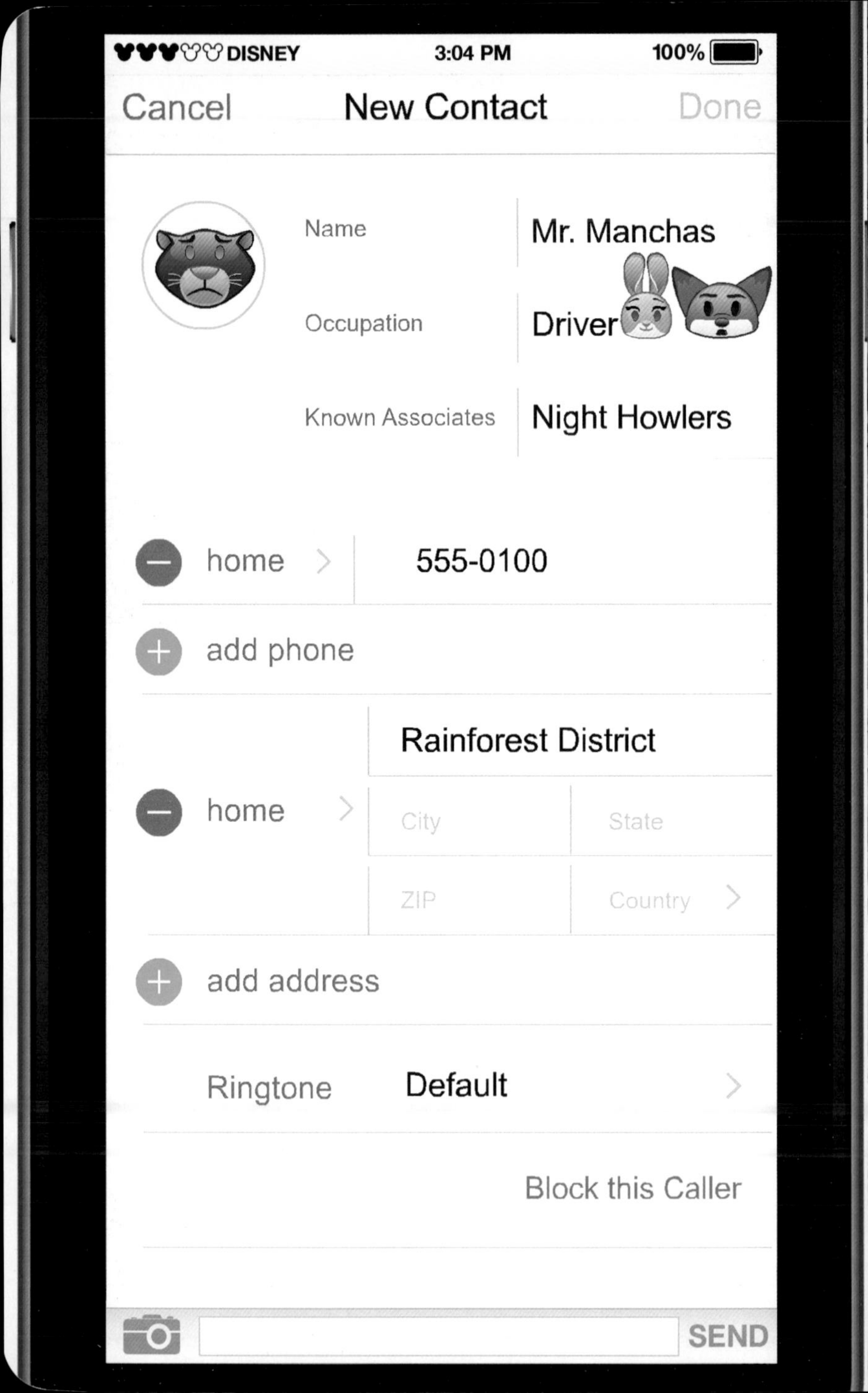
DISNEY
3:04 PM
100%
Cancel
New Contact
Done
Name
Mr. Manchas
Occupation
Driver
Known Associates
Night Howlers
home
555-0100
add phone
Rainforest District
home
City
State
ZIP
Country
add address
Ringtone
Default
Block this Caller
SEND

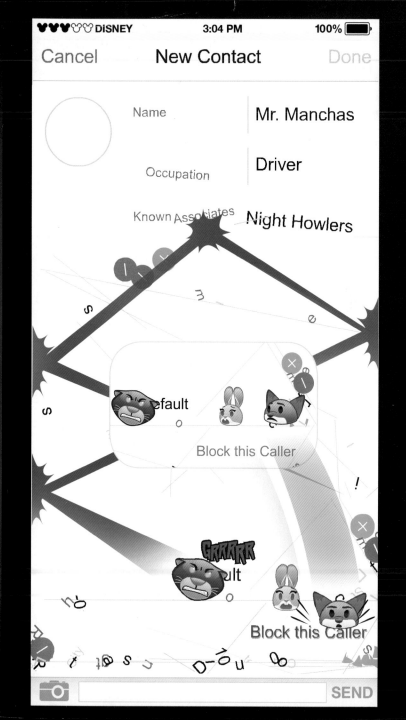

Cancel   **New Contact**   Done

Name   Mr. Manchas

Occupation   Driver

Known Associates   Night Howlers

efault

Block this Caller

GRRRR

ult

Block this Caller

SEND

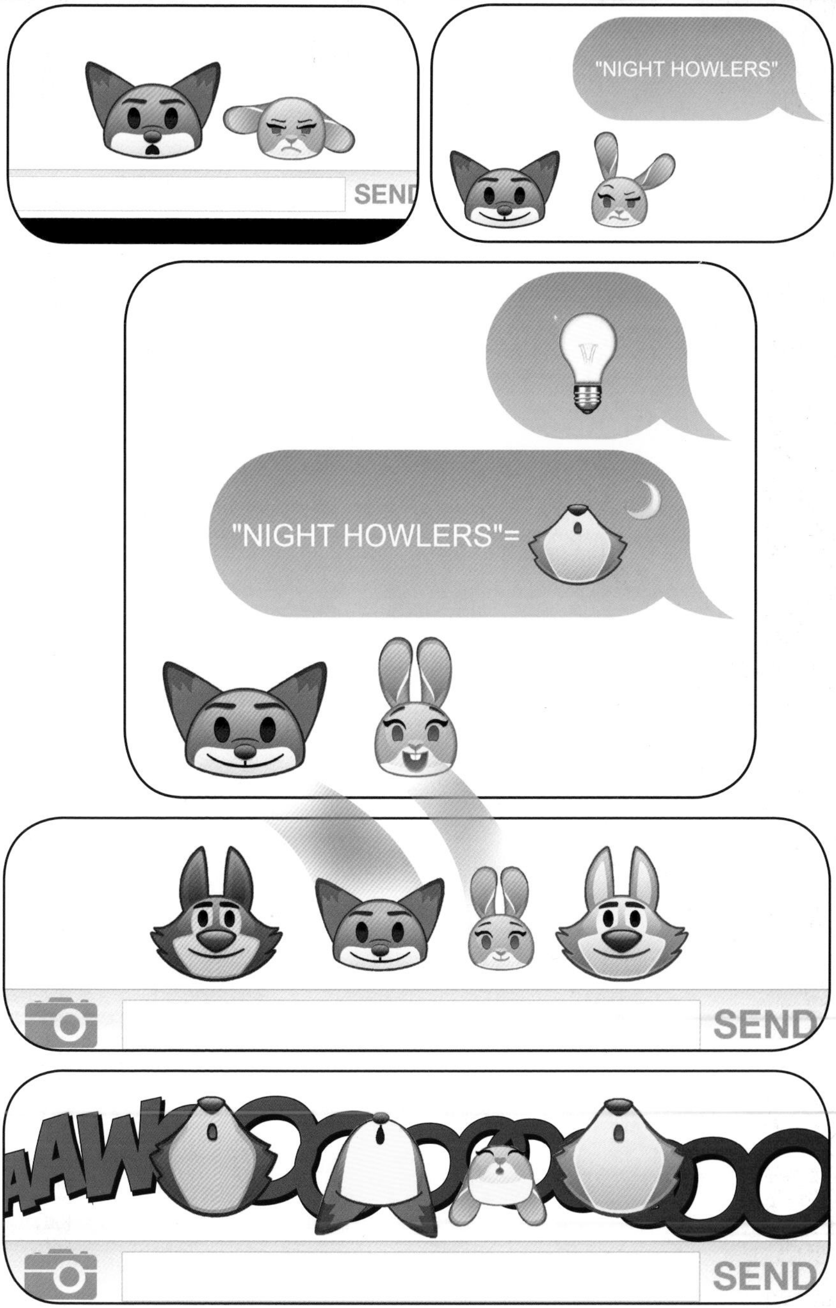
SEND
"NIGHT HOWLERS"
"NIGHT HOWLERS"=
SEND
SEND

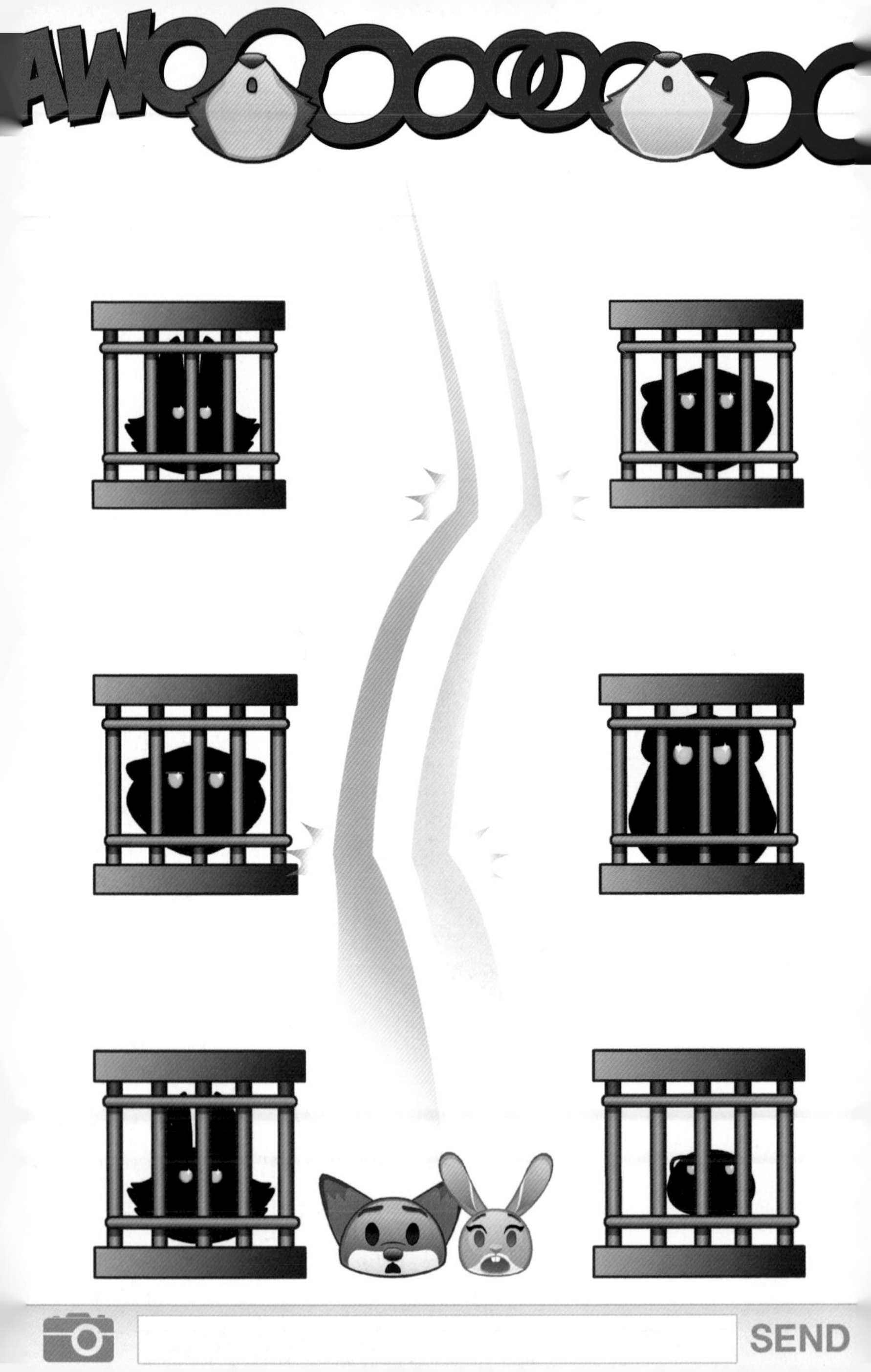
AWOOOOOOOOO
SEND

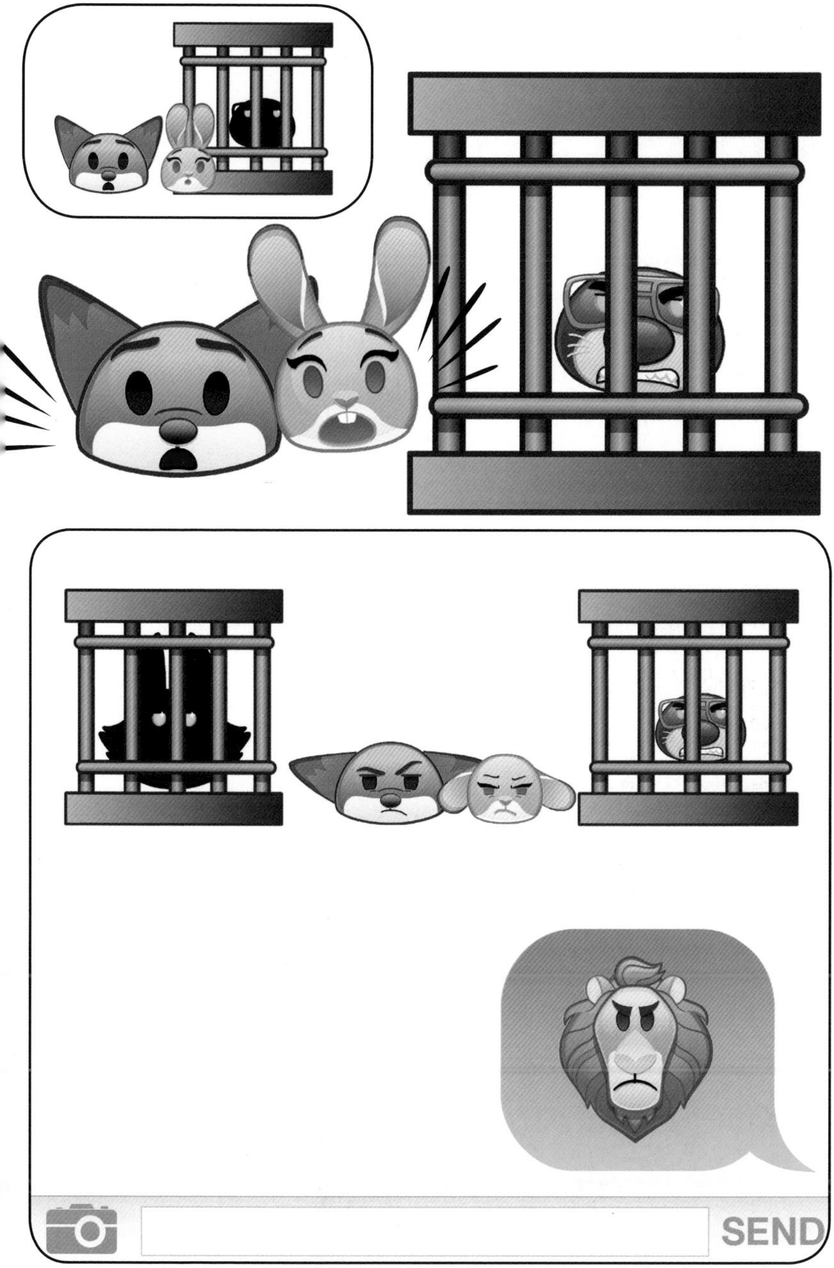
SEND

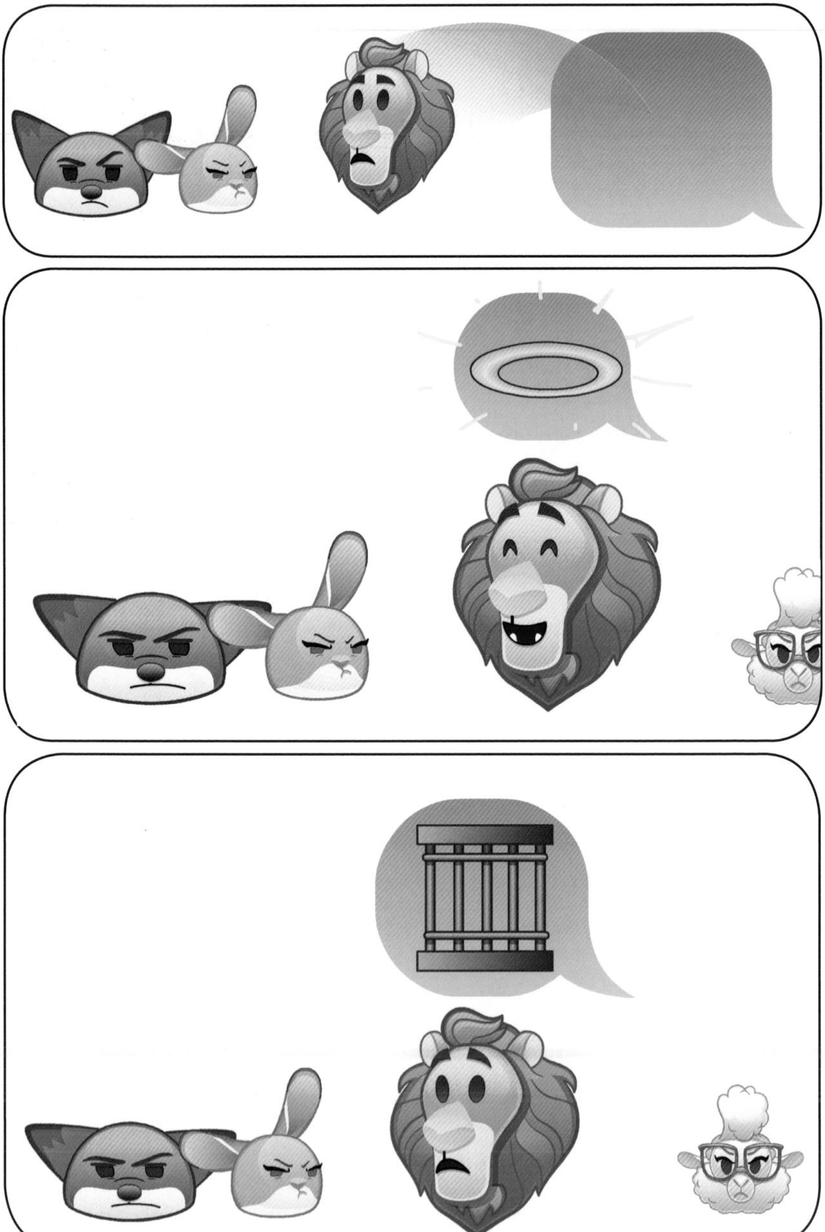

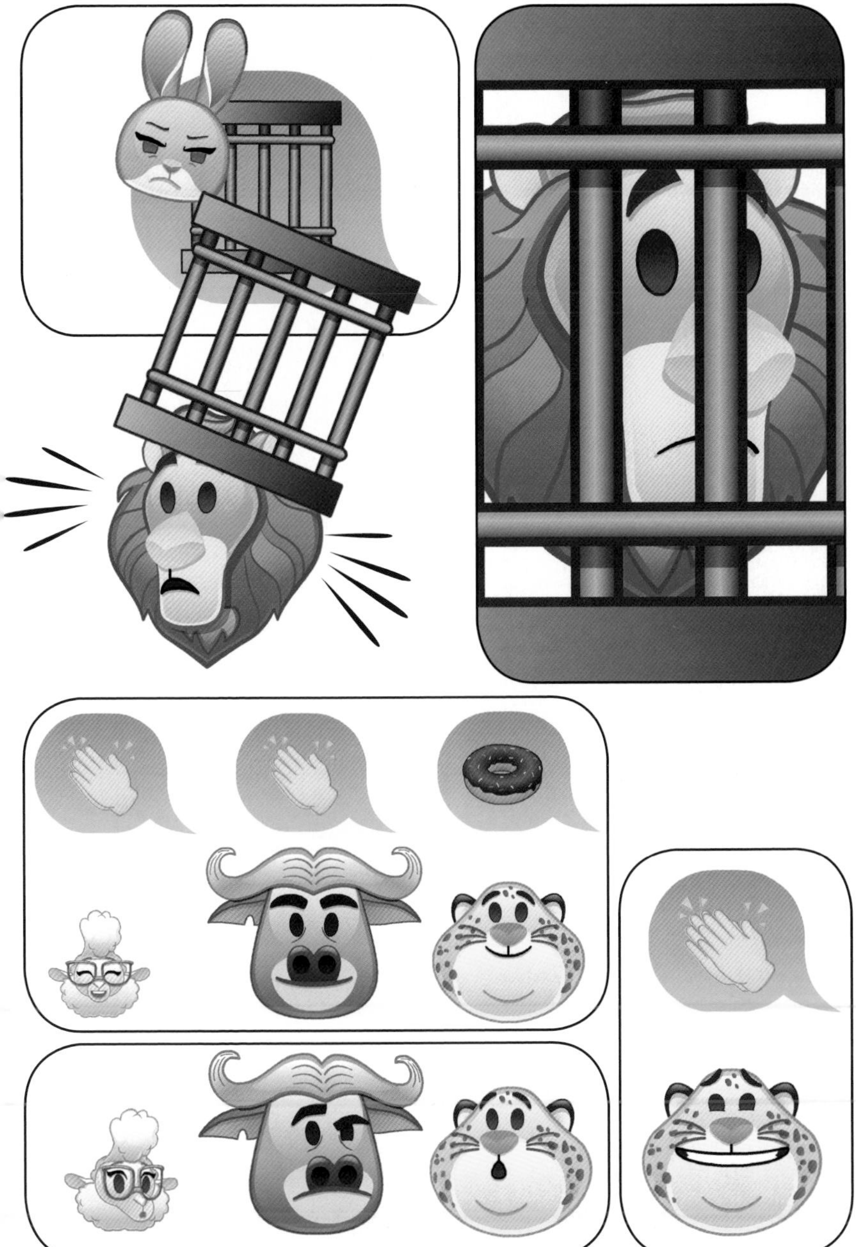

Judy holds a press conference to explain how she cracked the case

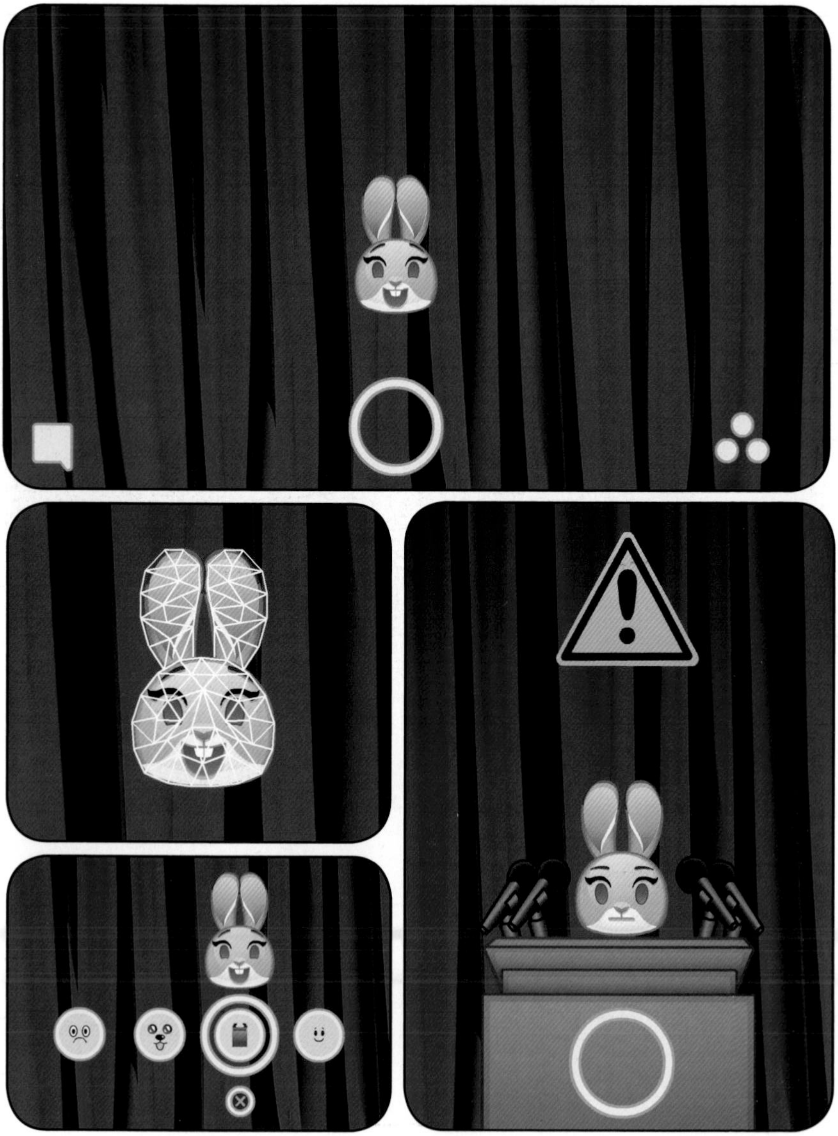

But she accidentally offends all the predators of Zootopia...

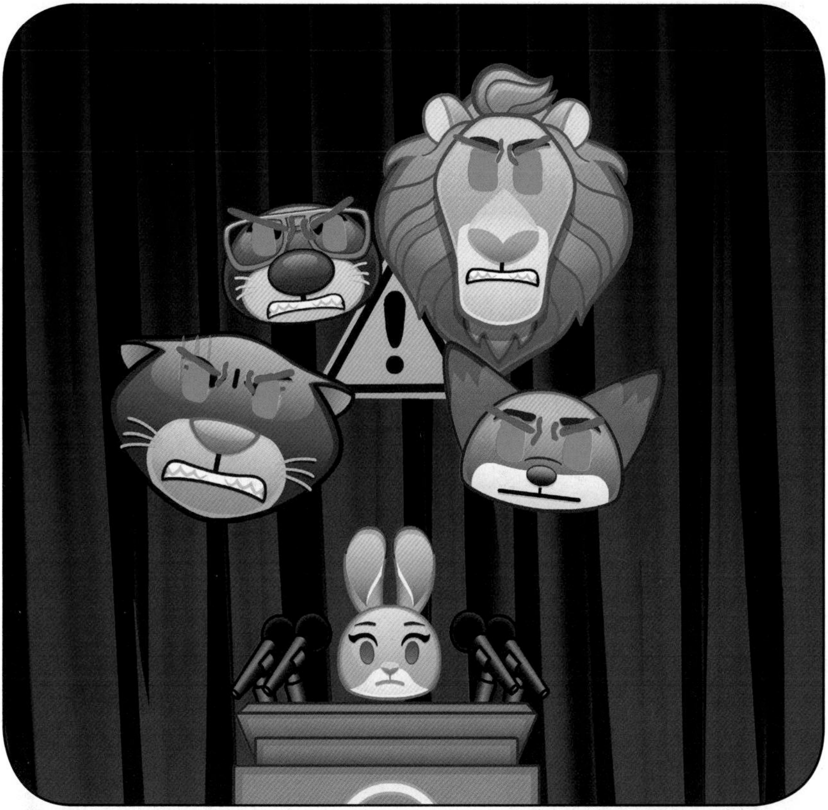

Especially Nick

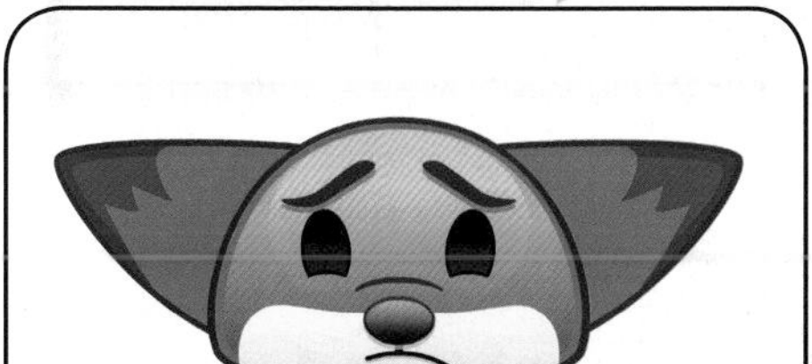

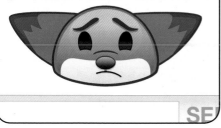

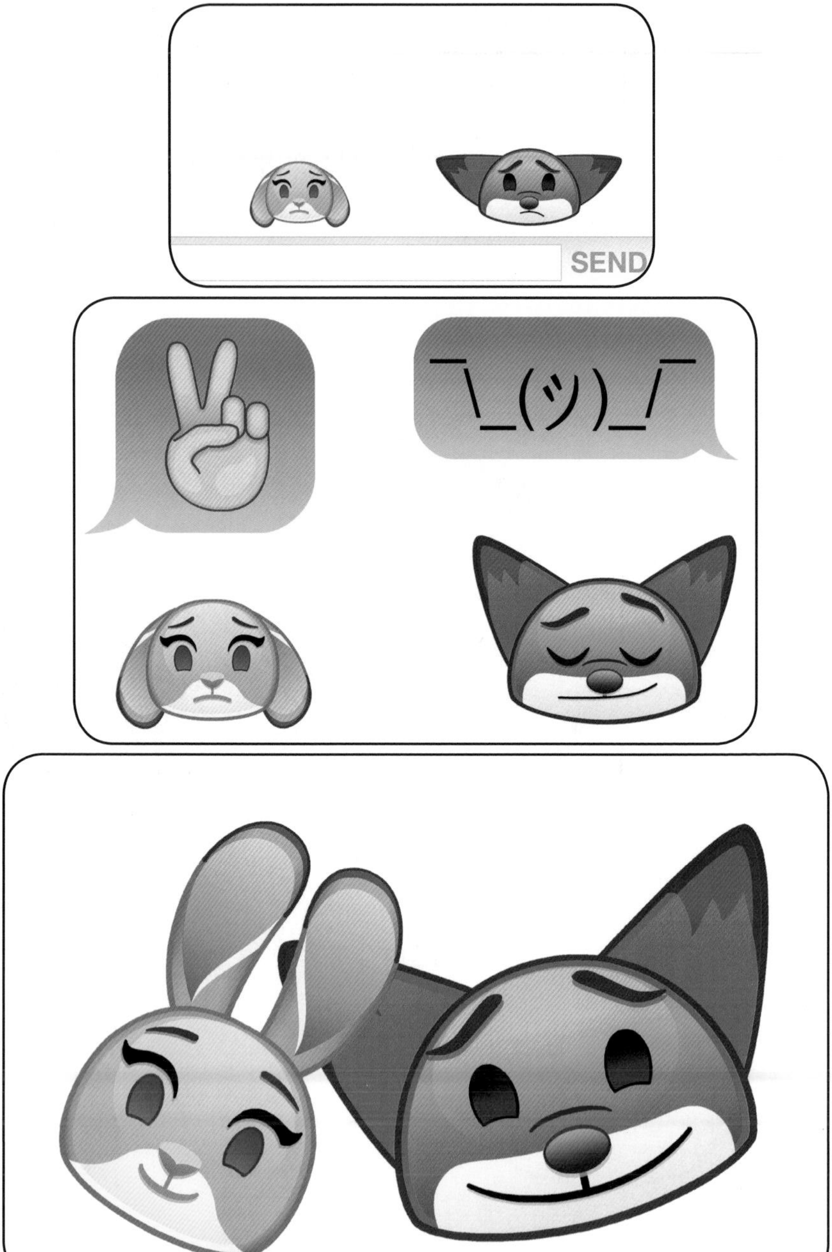
SEND
¯_(ツ)_/¯

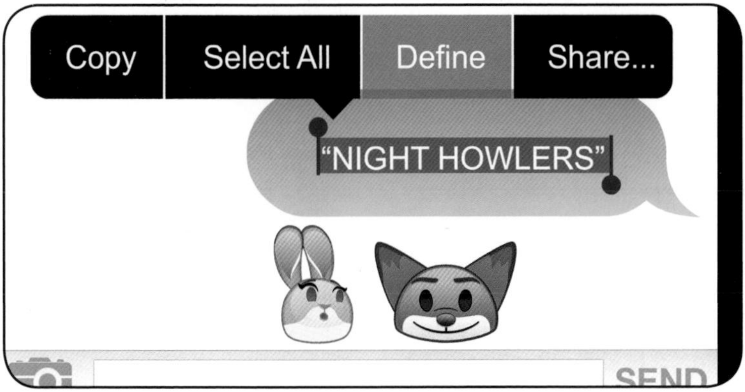
Copy
Select All
Define
Share...
"NIGHT HOWLERS"
SEND

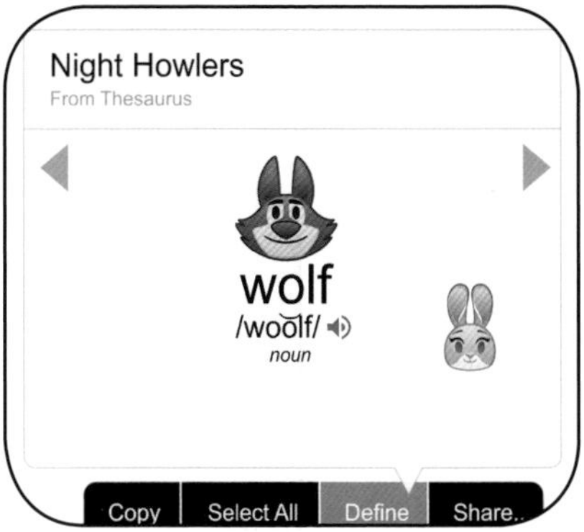
Night Howlers
From Thesaurus
wolf
/wo͝olf/
noun
Copy
Select All
Define
Share..

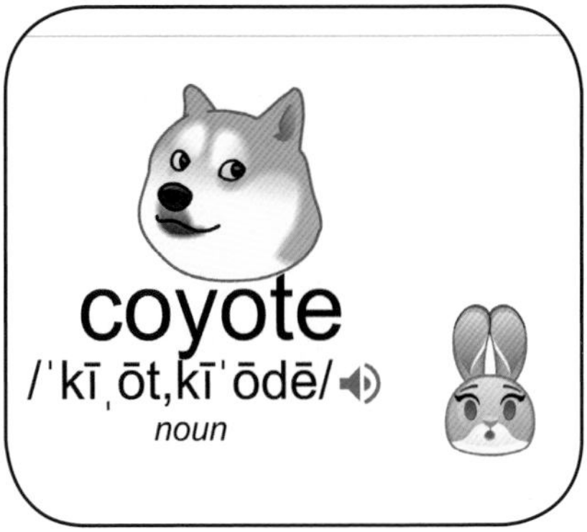
coyote
/ˈkīˌōt,kīˈōdē/
noun

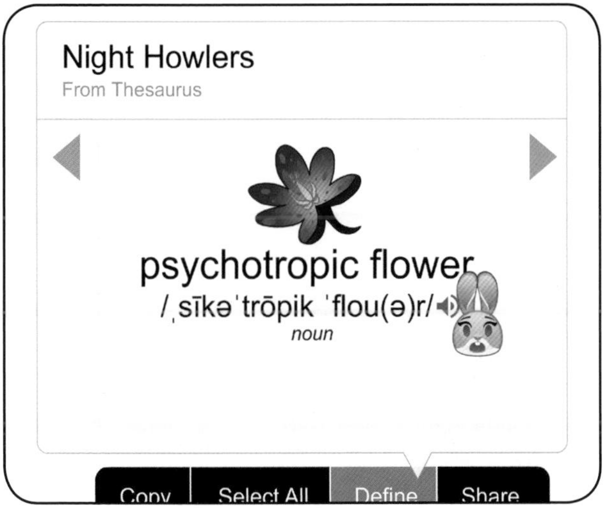
Night Howlers
From Thesaurus
psychotropic flower
/ˌsīkəˈtrōpik ˈflou(ə)r/
noun
Copy
Select All
Define
Share

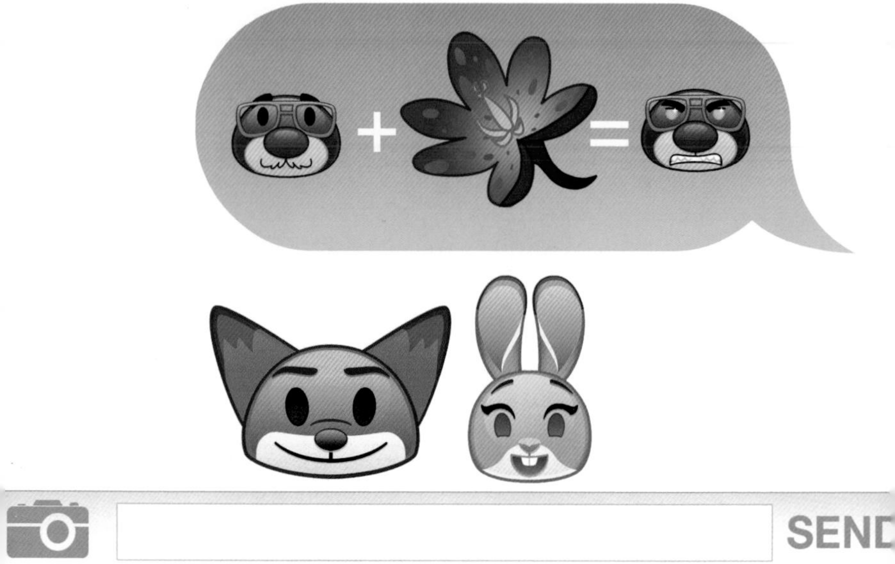
SEND

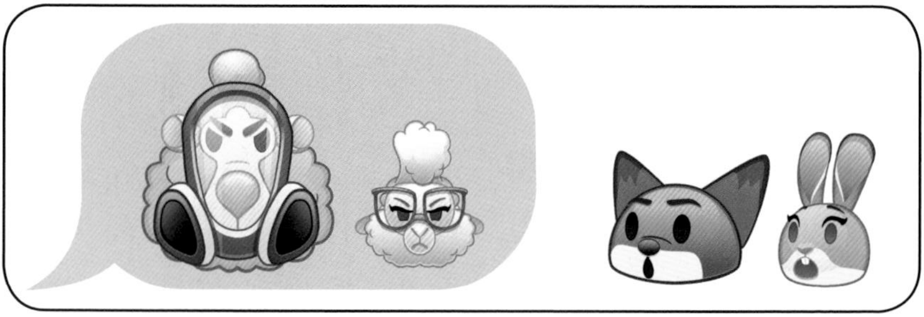

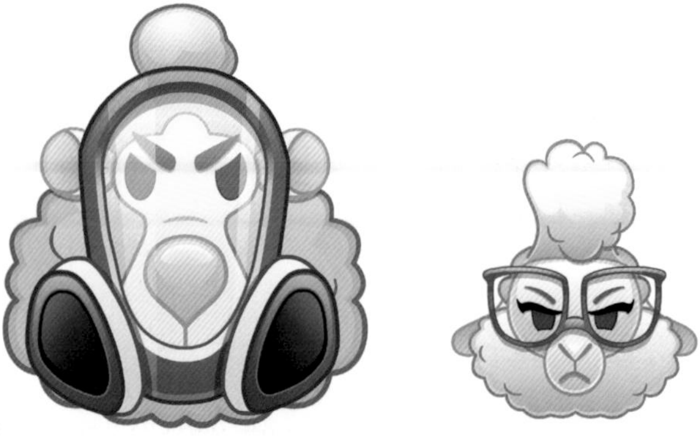

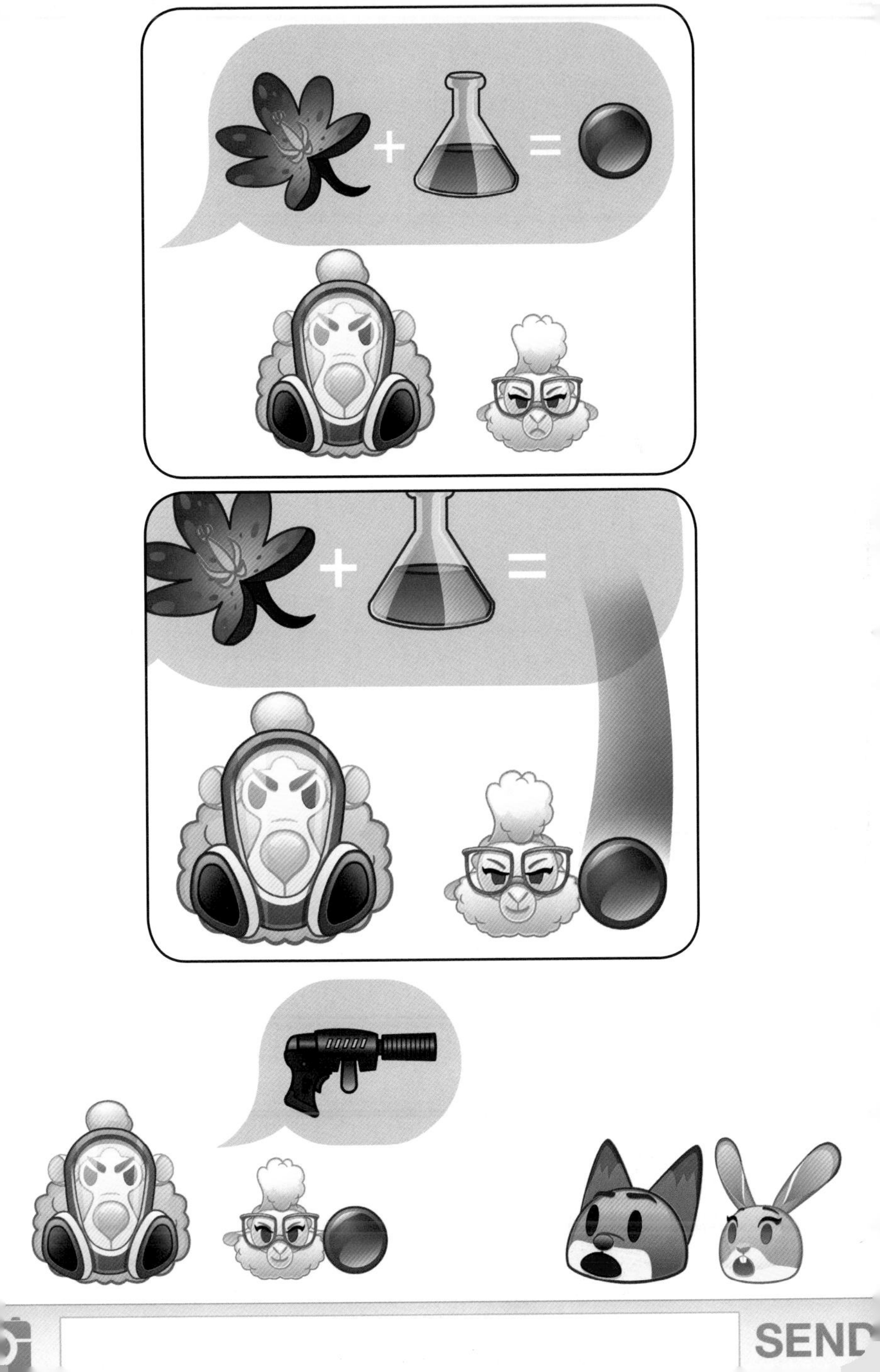
SEND

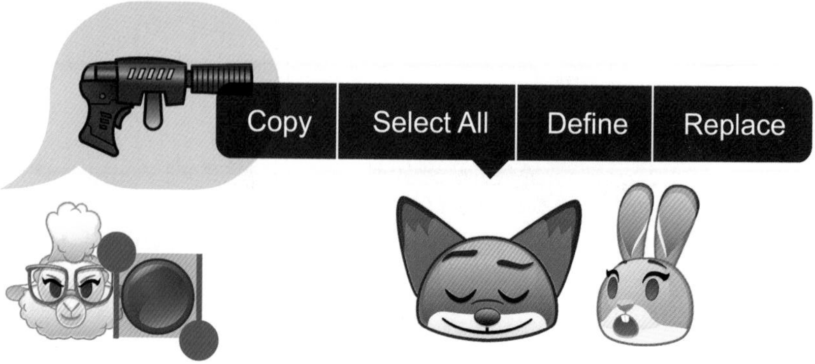
Copy
Select All
Define
Replace

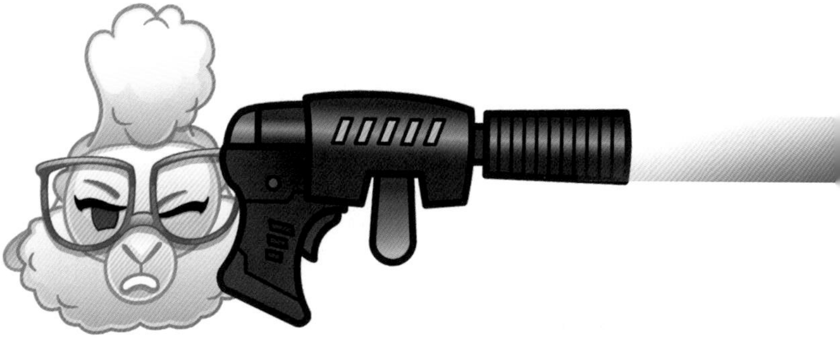

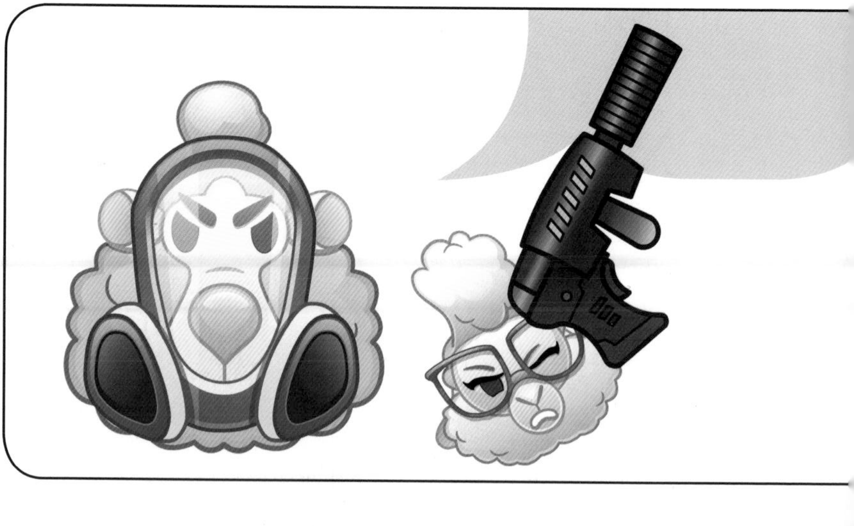

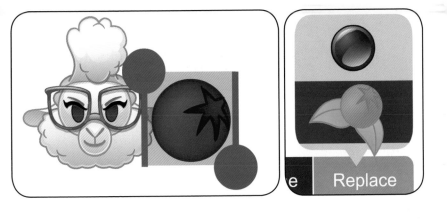

Replace

SPLAT

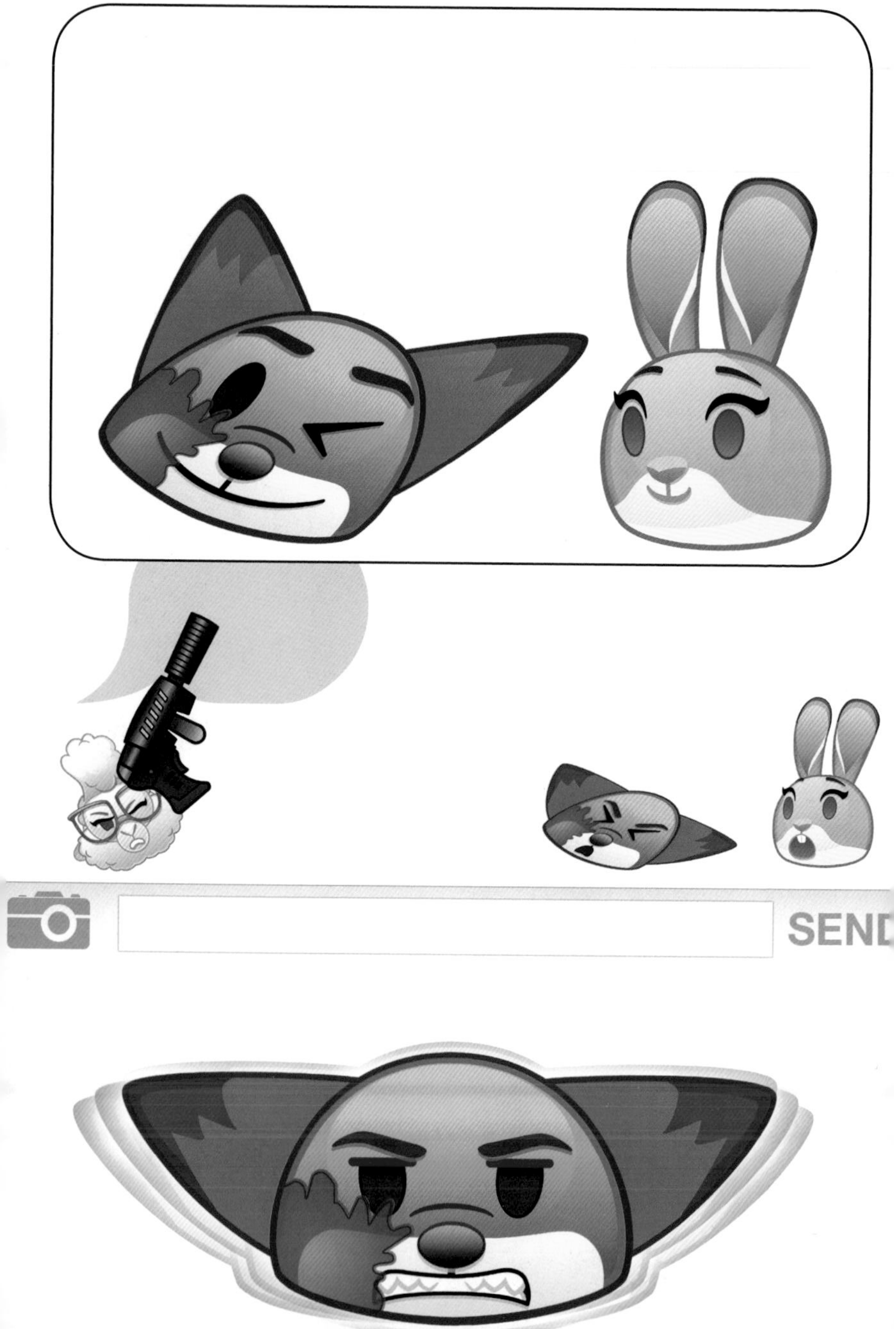
SEND

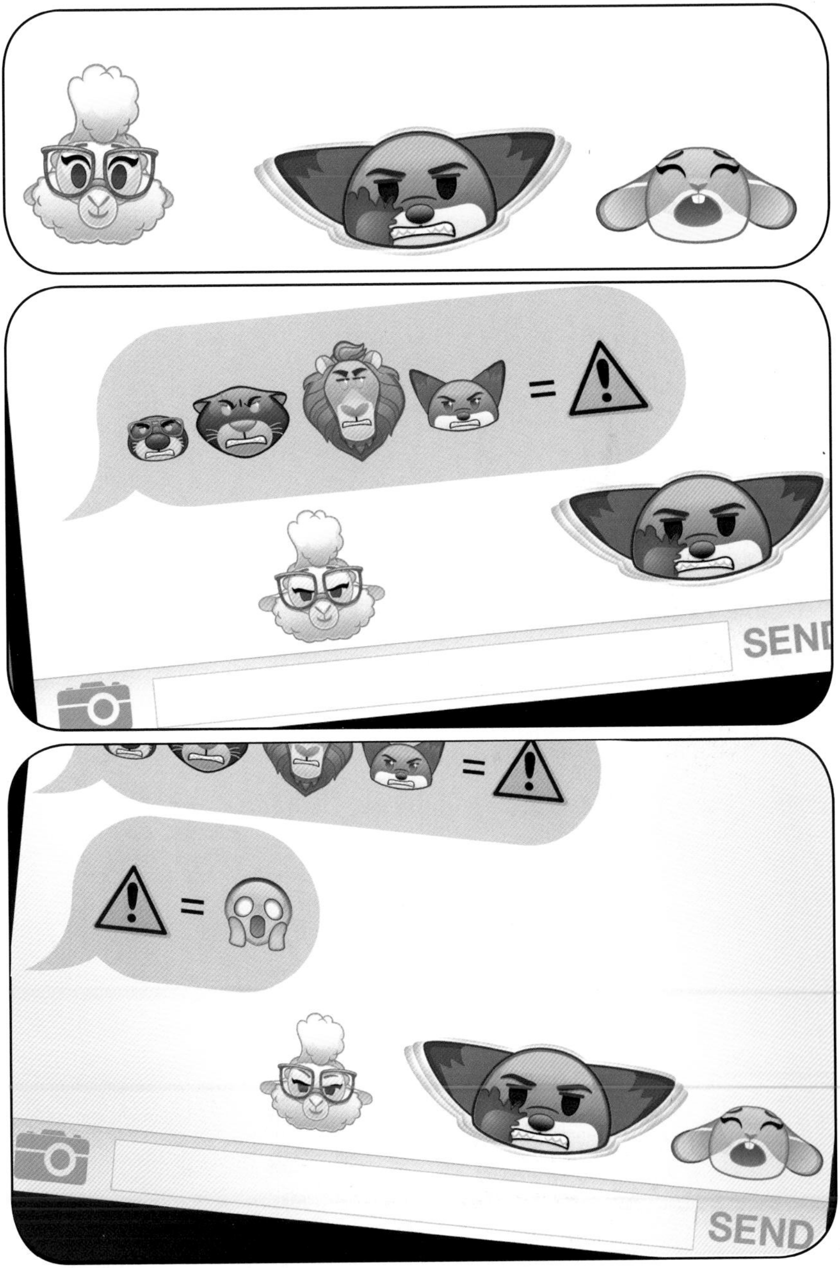
SEND

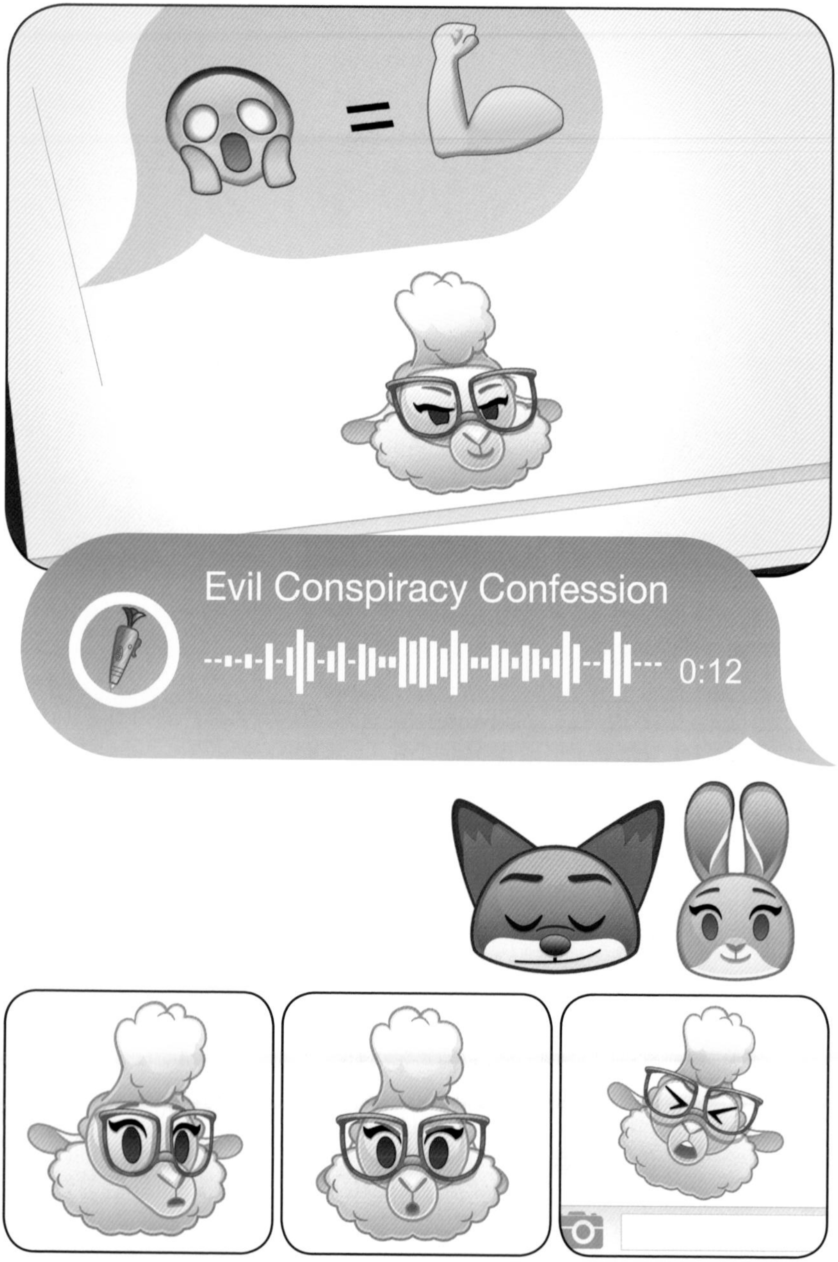
Evil Conspiracy Confession
0:12

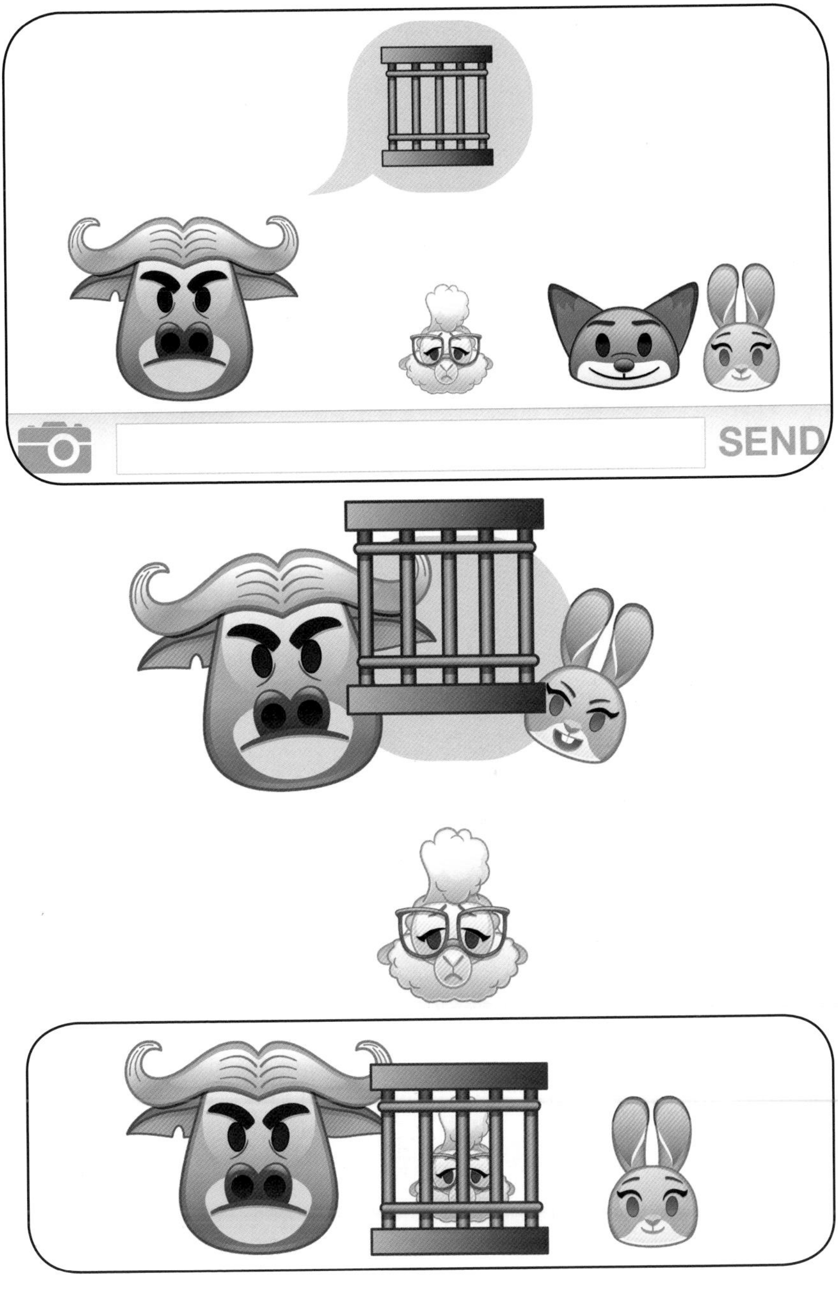
SEND

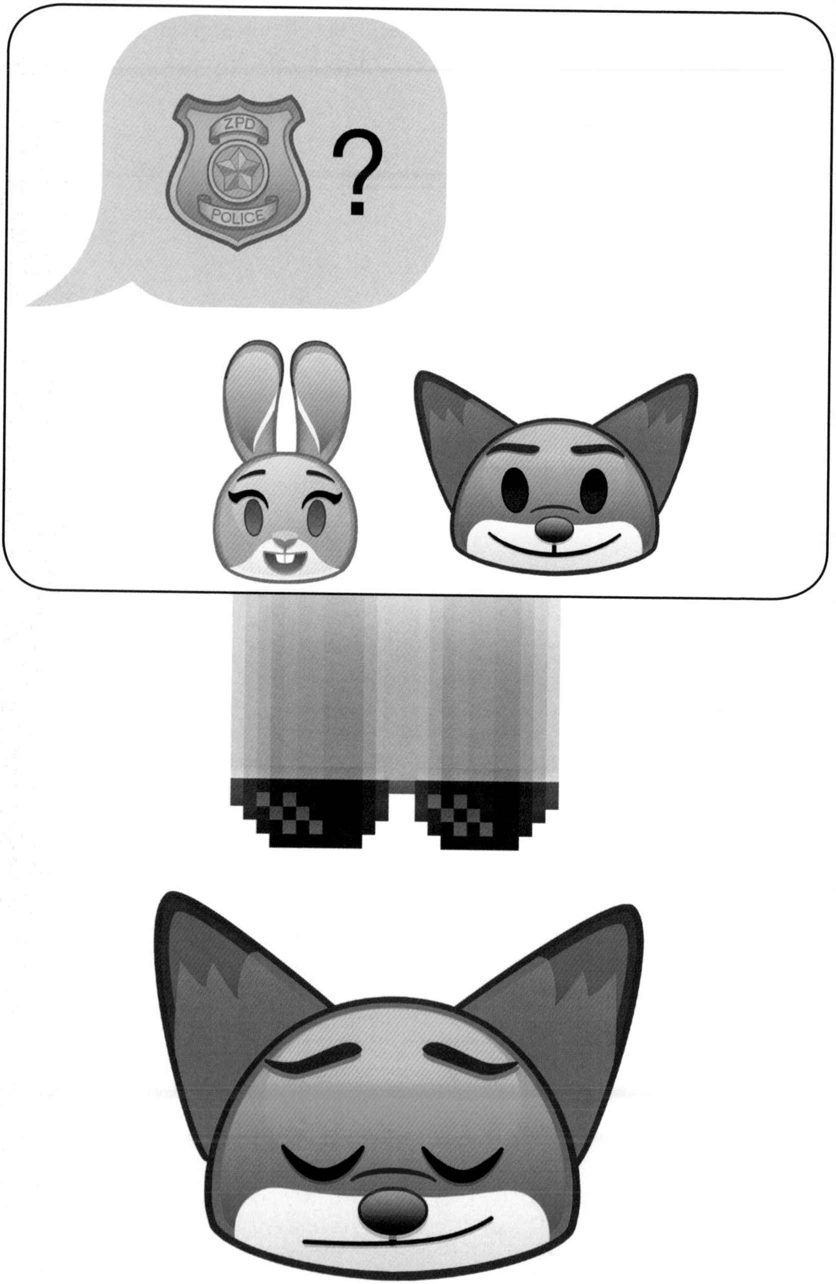
ZPD
POLICE
?

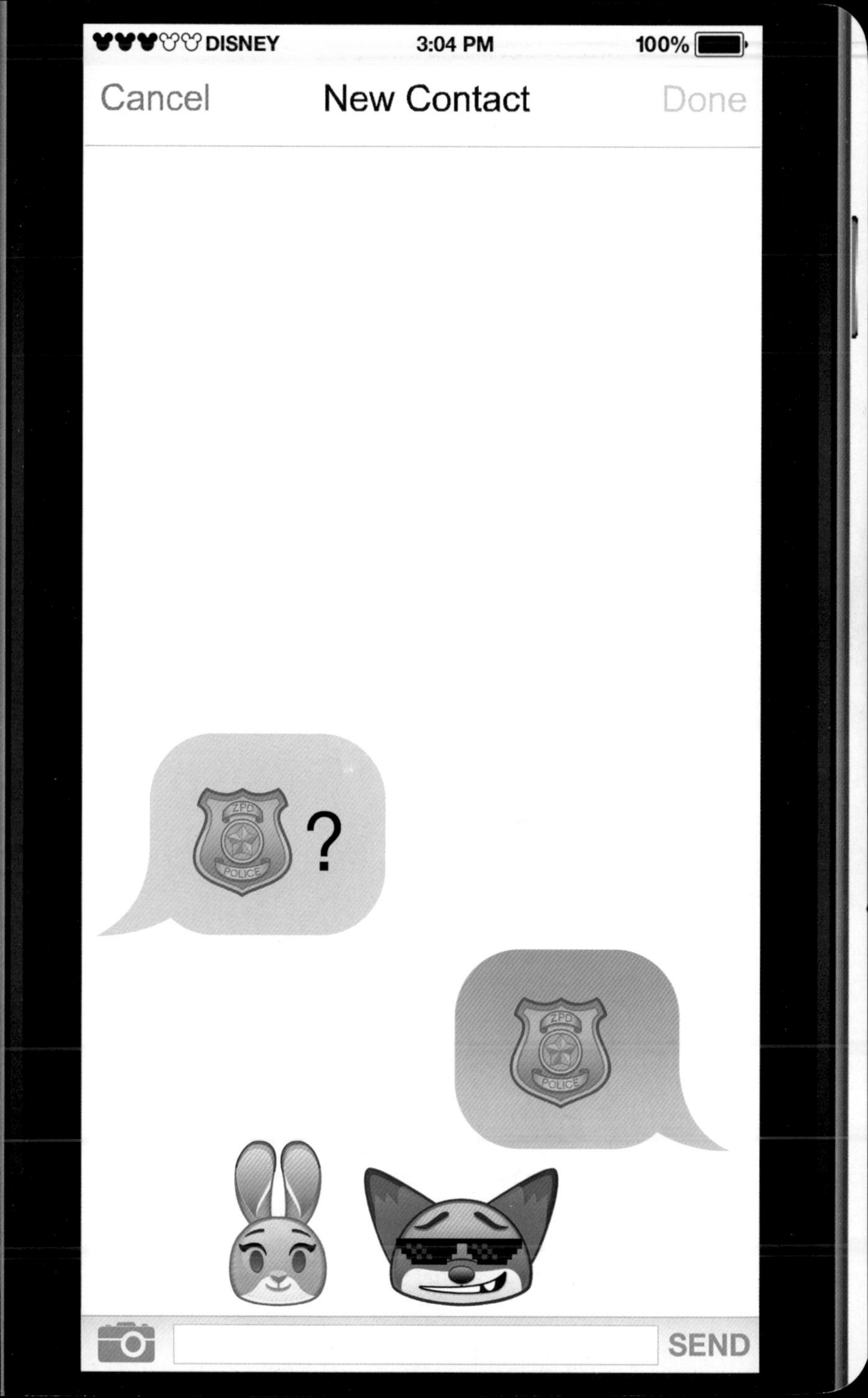
DISNEY
3:04 PM
100%
Cancel
New Contact
Done
ZPD
POLICE
?
ZPD
POLICE
SEND

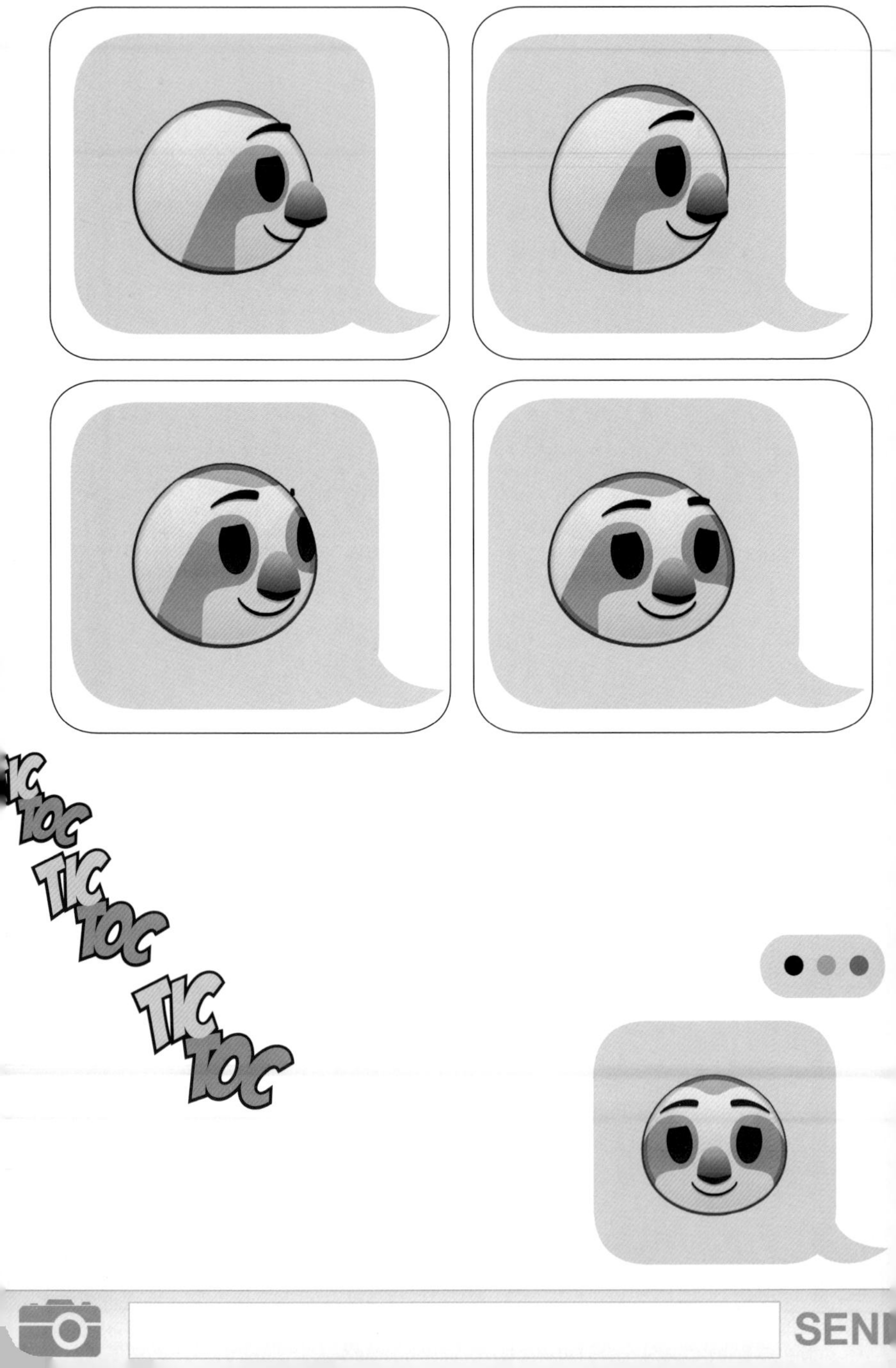
TOC
TIC
TOC
TIC
TOC

THE END.

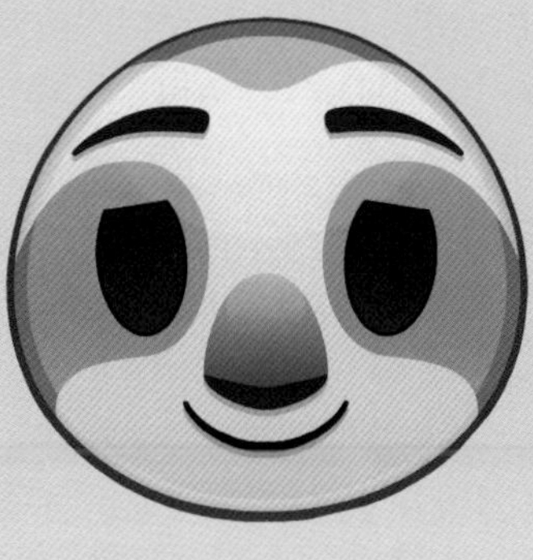

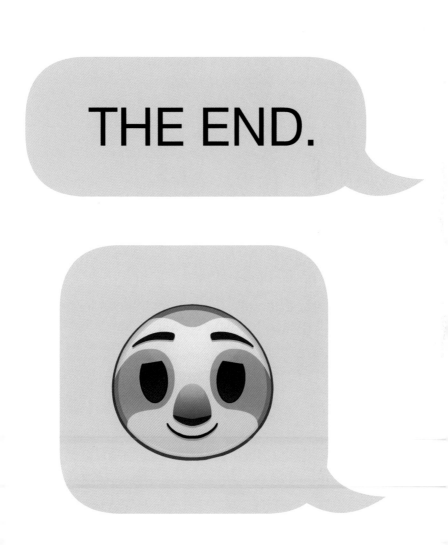

Judy Hopps

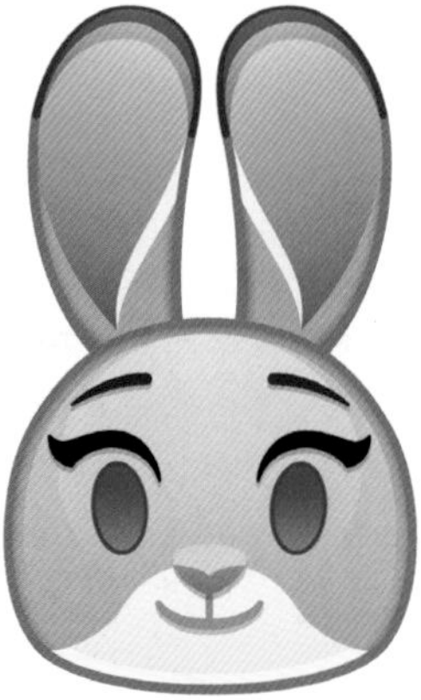

Idealistic Judy Hopps is the first bunny ever to earn her  from Zootopia's police department.

Determined to prove herself,  jumps at the chance to crack a case, even if it means teaming up with a con-artist .

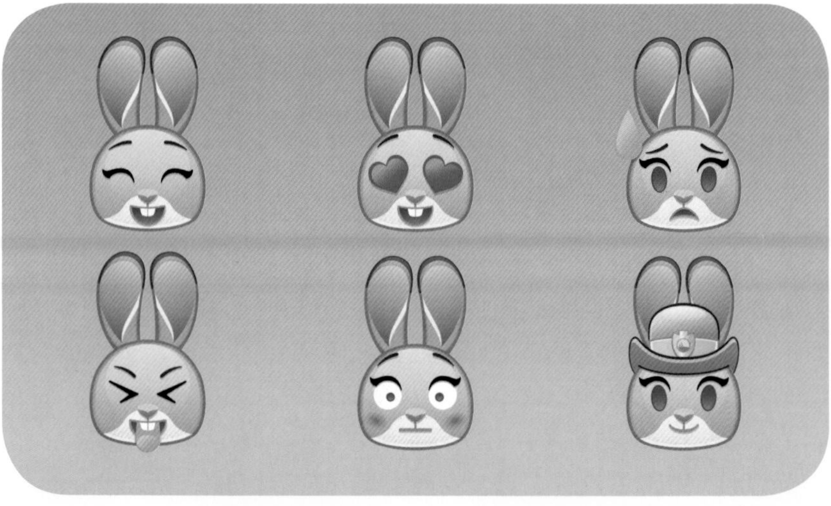

Nick Wilde

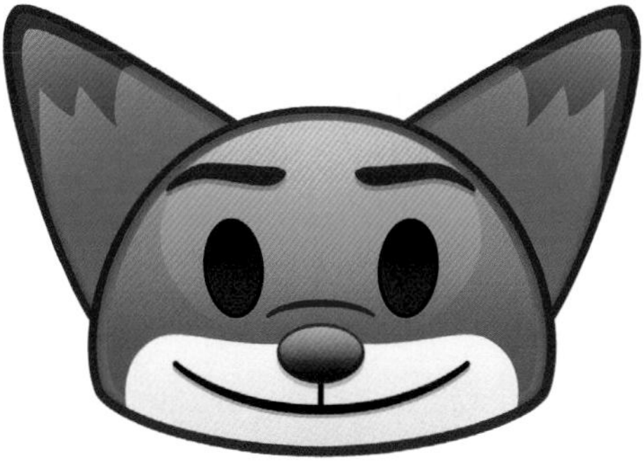

Nick Wilde is a charming, small-time con-artist fox with  on his mind and a lot of opinions.

But when  outsmarts him,  finds himself actually helping her solve a mystery.

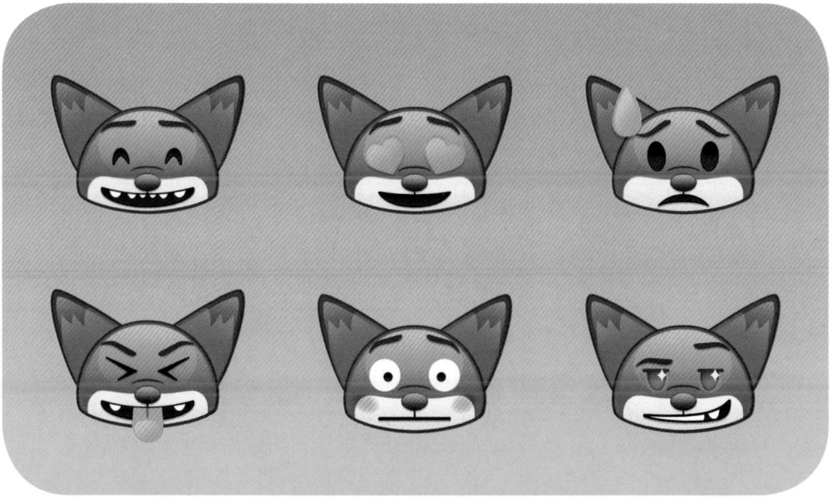

Chief Bogo

A tough Cape buffalo, Chief Bogo is the chief of 🛡️.

🐃 will give credit where credit is due—but he doubts that 🐰 will ever be able to prove herself.

Officer Clawhauser

Officer Benjamin Clawhauser is Zootopia Police Department's most charming cheetah.

 loves pop star Gazelle and  .

Mayor Lionheart

Mayor Leodore Lionheart is the noble leader of Zootopia.

🦁 coined the city's mantra, which 🐰 lives by: "In Zootopia, anyone can be anything."

Assistant Mayor Bellwether

Assistant Mayor Bellwether is a sweet sheep with a little voice and a lot of wool.

🐑 constantly finds herself underfoot of the larger-than-life 🦁.

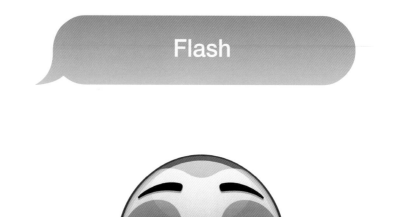

Flash is the fastest sloth working at the DMV—of course, that's not saying much.

When his pal 😼 needs a rush job, 😴 springs into action (as much as a sloth can spring, anyway).

Collect them all!

As Told By
Disney emoji

Disney
Tim Burton's
The Nightmare Before Christmas
As Told By
Disney emoji
CINESTORY COMIC

Disney
Beauty and the Beast
As Told By
Disney emoji
CINESTORY COMIC

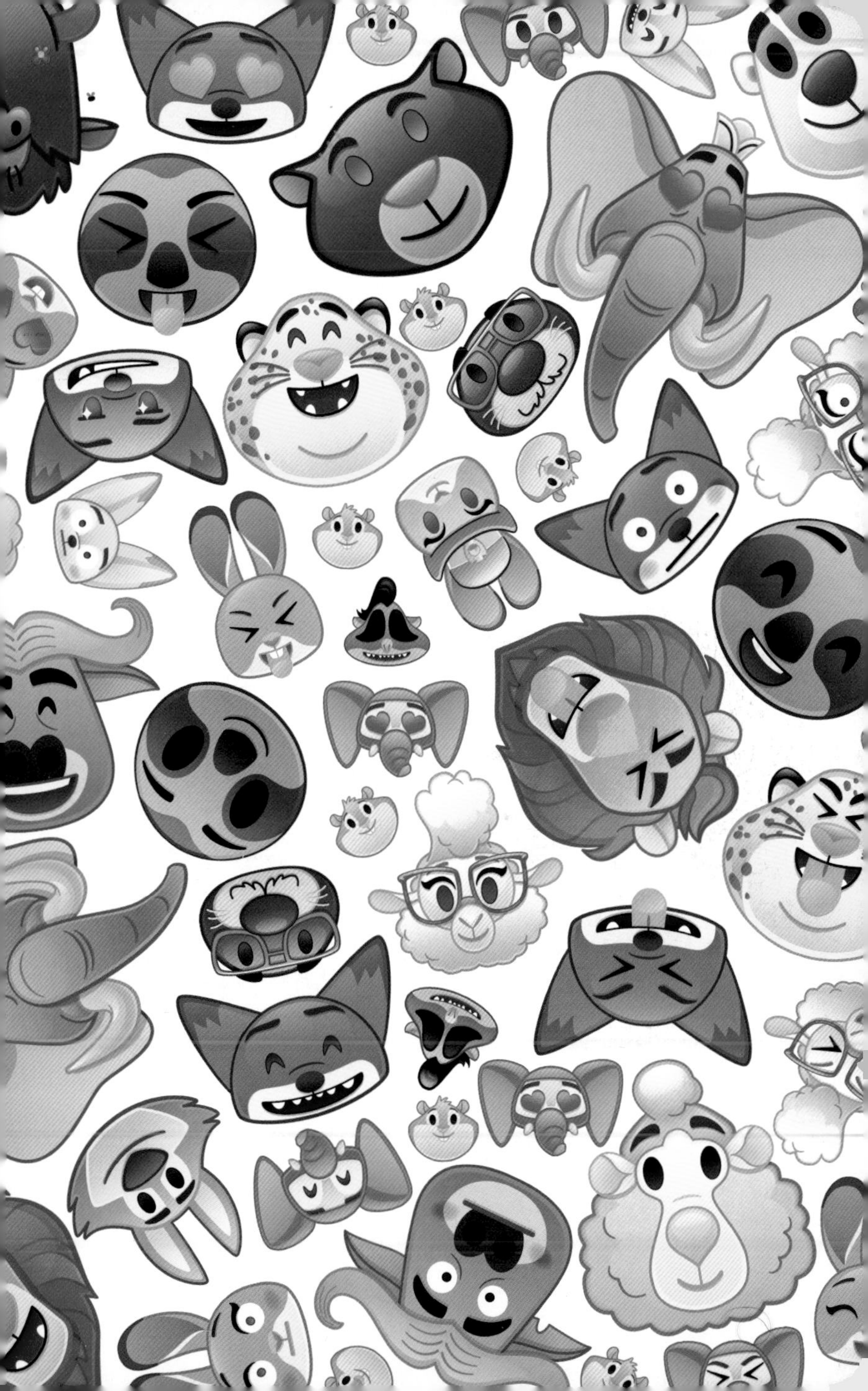

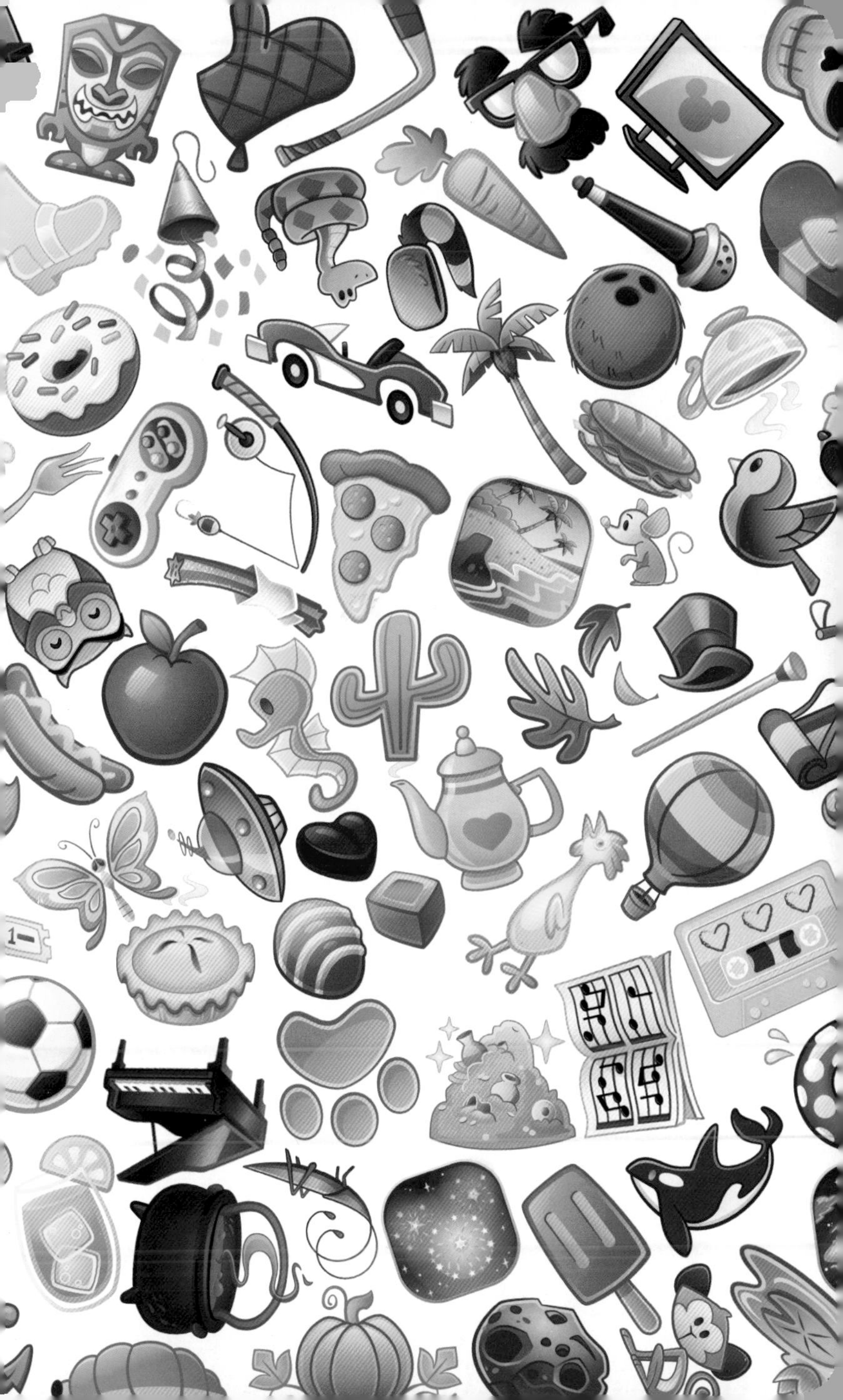

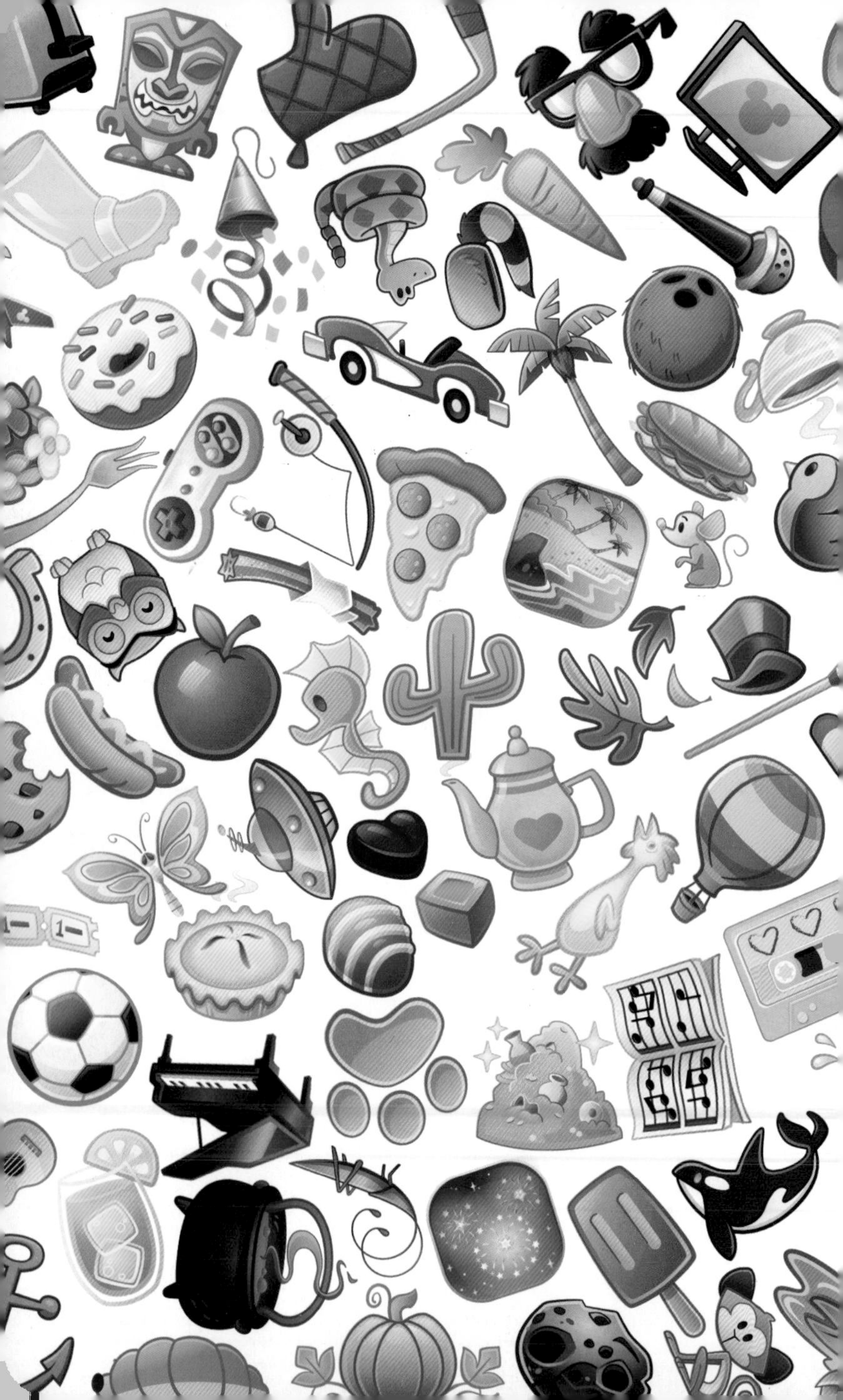